Cricket's Craziest Crime

One Night, One Game, Twenty Million Dollars

Paragon Publishing

If you enjoy this book, then please leave us a review on amazon. We are a small publishing company so any feedback is greatly appreciated.

from various sources. Please consult a licensed professional before attempting any techniques outlined in this book.

By reading this document, the reader agrees that under no circumstances is the author responsible for any losses, direct or indirect, that are incurred as a result of the use of the information contained within this document, including, but not limited to, errors, omissions, or inaccuracies.

Contents

Introduction

On the 11th of June 2008, the world of cricket changed forever under the sound of whirling rotary blades, a broad smile, and a Perspex box filled with $20 million. Lord's Cricket Ground—or simply, Lord's—had been the Mecca of cricket since 1814. Throughout that time, it had garnered a reputation as a place where morals, manners, and decency were not just expected, but they were demanded.

To the people who play there, it is hallowed turf, a stadium like no other, and a place where legends are made and praised. History almost seems to seep up through the grass, and a dress code applies to all who wish to enter. Apart from playing host to Middlesex County Cricket Club (MCCC) since 1877, Lord's is also the home of the England and Wales Cricket Board (ECB) and the European Cricket Council (ECC). It is a place of worship to the die-hard cricket fans, and to most, it is the one ground in the world where class and dignity should always reign supreme.

So, as the deafening sound of a chopper overhead ripped through the summer air, most of the locals would have presumed the last place it would land would be inside Lord's. But it did, and as the whirring blades slowed down, Allen Stanford's company logo could be seen clearly on the bodywork as it glistened in the afternoon sun.

When a brash, tall Texan stepped out of the black helicopter onto the turf of the Nursery End, those who had believed in the sanctity of all things Lord's might have been forgiven for rubbing their eyes and taking a second glance. He wore a ludicrously oversized jacket, his greying hair shone against his deep tan, and he walked with the confidence of a man who knew he had billions in the bank. Whether that money he so desperately wanted people to know he had was actually his would remain to be seen, but right at that moment, a little piece of cricket was dissolved forever in a wave of American glitz.

He was offering something that cricket—and almost any other sport in history—had never seen. The idea that $20 million could be placed on one match seemed like the stuff of Hollywood movies, and in a sense, it was. Along with this insane prize fund, Stanford was also offering an extra $80 million over a 5-year period in a claimed attempt to bring the world of cricket—especially the West Indies—to the forefront of the sporting world.

Maybe it was this $80 million rather than the $20 million the players would receive that appealed to the cricket board? Whatever the case may be, they now believed the lure of the recently formed—and much more lucrative—Indian Premier League (IPL) might not seem as tempting to their top young British talents as it reportedly was. But cricketers are not like footballers or basketball players who need half a million a week just to get out of bed, and the history and pride of the game are always the most important thing, so this sort of gimmick was nearly sacrilege.

For the reporters and cricket fans in attendance, one of the biggest shocks would have been the way this relatively unknown billionaire was greeted by the higher-ups and the cricket board. Stanford was fawned over, and his arrogant, brash nature was blatantly ignored. It seemed the idea of such a large cash injection into a sport that England had been falling behind in was too much to turn down.

For the likes of England cricket chief David Collier and ECB Chairman Giles Clarke, the stain left by the whole Stanford debacle would never fully wash out, but at the time, they seemed more than happy to welcome him. Money has a way of making people turn a blind eye—at least for those with their hands in the pot—but even so, they must have known the risks of getting involved with a man like Stanford.

Although, despite Stanford's previous shady dealings before that day in 2008 (we'll get into them later!), he had garnered a somewhat surprising proven track record where funding cricket was concerned. The Stanford 20/20 (yes, he called the competition after himself) in the Caribbean had been a roaring success. Both tournaments in 2006 and 2008 were widely successful, and there were records of Stanford pumping money that was to be used to help cricket grow at a grassroots level in at least 20 of the islands.

Of course, his severe lack of knowledge of the sport would become evident after he had spoken a few words, but if Allen Stanford had one quality, it was his passion for the things he was promoting and investing in.

Everyone who met him spoke of a man with charisma, hyper-masculinity, and an infectious drive. That he was bestowing these traits on crooked schemes and money laundering is another matter, but one thing was for sure—when Allen Stanford said he was going to do something, he meant business.

Now, we need to remember that in 2008, English cricket was in a state of decline. Well, that might not be a fair statement, but they certainly were being left behind by other nations. The IPL had just completed its maiden season, and it had been massively successful. Many of Britain's top talents were already being tempted by the higher pay cheque, the fame, and the excitement the IPL had to offer, and there was genuine worry among the ECB that some of the players might switch over.

Having $20 million to share between a winning England side for one game would have been seen as a great incentive for the players to stay where they were, and this was probably one of the main aspects that led to the ECB turning a blind eye to Stanford's past. That, or they weighed up the pros and cons and decided that, well, the Texan's money was a hell of a lot heavier than his previous exploits.

Along with the rousing success of the IPL, the Stanford 20/20—despite the ridiculous name—had genuinely made waves in the world of cricket. English cricket was lagging, and many ex-professionals, including Sir Ian Botham and Sir Viv Richards, believed the stuffed-shirt approach of the British cricket boards needed to be reconsidered. Nobody was asking the ECB to introduce pom-pom-waving cheerleaders and entrance music, but the general feeling was that they could do with opening their minds at least a little.

Whether the answer lay inside a tacky Perspex box filled with $20 bills is another question. In hindsight, the ECB made quite a leap after their original trepidation towards glamorising their sport. That word 'hindsight' will come into play a lot throughout the story of Allen Stanford, as much of what he offered the world —not just cricket—seemed a whole lot more appealing on the surface. Just like the Perspex box he presented at Lord's, once the outer layer of notes was removed, the centre was nothing but stuffing and fake promises.

It must also be remembered that plans to bring cricket to a broader audience had already been put into place before Stanford's preposterous helicopter landing on the pitch of the Nursery End, and it was the English who had made the decision. The introduction of the Twenty20 in 2003 would have been unthinkable back in the classic years of cricket when leaf-strewn pitches and crumpets were aplenty, but the almost instant global appeal it garnered changed the minds of even the most cynical cricket fans.

The sport was changing, and it felt like the only nation that hadn't bought a ticket to the ride was Britain. Letting a clearly un-vetted Texan, who decades before had filed for bankruptcy and fled the United States, to be the man to run the carousel probably wasn't the best decision the ECB ever made. Still, once they had made their bed, they unfortunately had to sleep in it, and no amount of scrubbing themselves with Brillo pads would ever completely get the stench of what happened off them.

Stanford claimed the game between England and the Stanford Superstars (yes, he named the team after himself too!) was going to be the most extraordinary event in cricket history. Given the centuries of memories, magical moments, and stature the sport had built up, this sort of statement should have been a blatant red flag. But a $100 million investment will rose-tint most people's glasses, and the ECB and ECC were no different in that regard.

Not long after the infamous pitch-landing, a defiant Sir Ian 'Beefy' Botham—a bona fide cricketing legend—told the English players and media to basically reel their necks in and take the game for what it was.

"It's a real bonus for the players, and one they should just go out there and enjoy," he told the press. "It's the same for both teams. Just stop whinging and get on with it" (Sportsmail, 2008).

Beefy's sentiments were echoed by several other legends of the game, although for the majority, the whole idea of the Stanford 20/20 was just too much to swallow. The idea that the players who took part would be selling their souls was being widely thrown around. Of course, it would have been a lot easier to judge them from the outside looking in, but for the young men such as

Kevin Pietersen and Andrew Flintoff, the idea of a million dollars each for one game would have been highly appealing.

Stanford himself was trying to promote it all as simply a springboard for a better and more lucrative sport in the long run.

"I see the Stanford 20/20 as a fantastic opportunity for the current teams in the Stanford 20/20 tournament to take a giant leap into the spotlight and gain exposure to top-class opposition," he told reporters at Lord's. "The Stanford 20/20 for 20 will be a highly anticipated event, not just because of the prize money, but because of the traditional friendly rivalry that exists between England and the West Indies" (sidbreakball, 2016).

Regardless of the scepticism of almost everyone in attendance that day at Lord's, the ECB signed a $100 million 5-year contract with Sir (we'll get to that too!) Allen Stanford. Again, we're dealing in hindsight, but looking back, it still seems crazy that such an event happened at all. It stank of corruption and lies, but as is often the case throughout history, money talks. And when that money is stacked on a pallet in a Perspex case, it somehow becomes even harder to resist.

Quite unbelievably, the image of a shiny black helicopter landing on the pitch at Lord's is just a drop in the ocean of outrageous events in the life of Allen Stanford. From his early life owning a chain of health clubs in Texas to spending $25 million on a single party, the story of the man who tried to destroy cricket is one of pure entertainment.

The Early Years

Born Robert Allen Stanford to parents James Stanford, an opportunistic businessman, and Sammie Stanford (née Conn) on the 24th of March 1950, the boy who would always prefer to go by his middle name was raised in the city of Mexia, Texas. At a time when the oil bubble was expanding beyond everyone's wildest dreams, the Lone Star State was a place where investors and new companies seemed to get rich almost instantly.

Although his father was a man who liked to consider himself a shrewd operator, Allen Stanford would claim many years later that he felt he had inherited his business acumen from his grandfather, Lodis Stanford. Long before little Allen was pulling at his mother's apron strings and attempting to trade one cookie for the price of two, Lodis Stanford had owned a pretty successful barber shop in Mexia in the 1930s, but much like his yet-to-be-born grandson, the money he made through this venture was never going to be enough.

When the Great Depression swept through Texas—and the whole of America—Lodis saw an opportunity. He sold his barber shop at a loss and used the money to invest in an insurance company which he simply named Stanford Insurance Company. According to Allen Stanford during an interview from his prison cell nearly a century later, Lodis Stanford had risked his entire life savings and, thus, his family's future on the investment. It was a story that moulded Allen into the risk-taker in business and in life that he was to become and the type of balls-to-the-wall attitude he would always be associated with.

Allen's parents divorced when he was nine years old, and he spent most of his time living with his mother. Of course, he would remain close with his father throughout his life, and they would work together on many business adventures, including James's stint on the board of Stanford Financial Group (SFG). Whether one led the other or both were equally as shady remains to be seen, but their escapades would become the stuff of big business lore.

Not much is known about Allen Stanford's early childhood, but his high school report cards were reported as mediocre at best. What is known is that he was brash (not surprising), arrogant (ditto), and so completely sure of himself to the point of being an egomaniac. Believing exams pointless and grades to be just a piece of paper, Allen had decided long before his college years that determination and confidence would always shine through in business, and to an extent, he had been right.

Many stories about Allen Stanford's college days have emerged through the years, with some of the most common being his love of young women in short skirts, his lies about being a football star, and his belief that one day he would be rich. One of the things he told people to impress them that actually was true was that he taught scuba diving to tourists, and this was something that would come in handy for him years later when he fled—or just emigrated, if you ask the man himself—to the Caribbean.

At six-foot-four, Allen was an intimidating man from his early adulthood. Loud, obnoxious, and in-your-face, he was popular among certain cliques while loathed by others. He was chalk and cheese, and to those who knew him back then, he didn't seem to care either way. What he had was a belief that he should always be in charge, and no matter what obstacles were put in front of him, Stanford felt he had the strength and forethinking to just plough right through them.

Stanford left Eastern Hills High School with little to no credentials, but his belief in himself never wavered. After finishing up his time in his Fort Worth school, he studied for a degree in finance at Baylor University, Waco, Texas. Again, he hardly shone in his time there either, but he did scrape through just enough to leave with a BA in 1974. Much like his grades in high school, Stanford would see these credentials as unimportant: What mattered in business was who you were, who you knew, and how you presented yourself.

While he was struggling to maintain his grades at Baylor, Allen found himself needing a place to live. Early in 1972, he answered an advert he saw on a college bulletin board offering a room in a house nearby the Baylor campus. It was here he would meet a young man by the name of Alan Davis, AKA James A. Davis, and their lives would become forever entangled from that day forth. Most of the time would be spent making millions of dollars between them, and by all accounts, they shared a well-rounded friendship. Of course, that would all change when the noose began to tighten in the late 2000s and right up until they turned on each other in court.

According to those who knew both men personally during those college years, Alan Davis was the polar opposite of his new roommate. Introverted, quiet, and calculated, it would be their contrasting strengths that combined so well years later. Davis saw Allen Stanford as someone to look up to, the type of brazen womanizer he so desperately admired but couldn't quite pull off —at least not right away! Stanford, in turn, saw Davis as the yin to his yang and someone he could always depend on, no matter how shady a deal got.

One story about the day they first laid eyes on each other involves a young Allen Stanford showing up at his door and introducing himself as his new roommate. No interview, no references, no problem. Stanford's self-assurance knew no bounds, and Alan Davis found it infectious from day one.

Another tale of Stanford's outrageous behaviour came out years later, in which he constantly told anyone who would listen that he was related to the founder of the famed Stanford University (SU) in California. Of course, when these claims became public knowledge, SU quickly quashed them. Whether anyone at Baylor actually believed these egregious claims that young Allen spouted as he minced around the college grounds is unknown. Still, given how convincing and confident Stanford could be, we have to assume at least a few people did.

Alan Davis remained in awe of Stanford throughout his life and even began having illicit affairs just like his mentor. To those who knew Davis way back when, these revelations decades later would have been a shock, as he had been known as a quiet, loyal young man. But as we mentioned a moment ago, Allen Stanford had a way of getting his claws into people, and he would always know when to stroke their ego as well as when to break their spirit.

Although they didn't go directly into business together, Stanford saw something in Davis, and the two young men remained in contact as they went their separate ways. Stanford would later admit he always had a feeling they would meet again somewhere down the road, and Davis echoed those sentiments himself.

While at college, Allen Stanford met his sweetheart and soon-to-be first wife, a beautiful young woman by the name of Susan. They would go on to have a daughter, who Stanford bestowed the stereotypically Texan name of Randi. Not much is known about Stanford's relationship with Susan in the early years, but given what would come out later in his life, we can assume she was a patient and forgiving woman at the very least.

As we now know, Stanford had at least four "outside wives", as they were referred to by those closest to him. All of this would

14

happen in his time on the Caribbean islands years later, but the fact that he would be so openly brazen about his infidelities only goes to prove how his mind worked. These outside wives and illegitimate children—the number of which is still unknown—were confirmed decades later by none other than his father.

"I felt for Susan", James Stanford told one reporter in an interview in 2009. "Him having all these outside wives and all these kids. I would never have approved of it all, but I found out after the fact" (Churcher, 2009).

Given how reckless and fame-hungry Allen Stanford was and is, we know surprisingly little about his personal life, at least when it comes to his wives and mistresses. Even though he would regularly attend sporting events or business meetings with his latest squeeze trailing behind, his minions would be under strict instructions never to ask him about them. Stanford thrived on creating an image rather than abiding by one, so his cheating nature and endless stream of children by many different women will come as little surprise.

Almost as soon as he graduated and stepped out the doors of Baylor into the hot, Texan sun, Allen Stanford immersed himself in real estate. Two of his friends, a couple named Toni and Ed Cook, had been struggling to keep their small fitness centre afloat. Being the early seventies, sculpting one's body wasn't yet seen as a priority, but times were quickly changing, and Stanford saw an opportunity.

At a time when gyms and fitness centres were nothing but rusty weights and medicine balls, Stanford quickly realised the potential for more elegant gyms of the likes of the movers and shakers on Wall Street were frequenting. He purchased the building from his friends, renamed it Total Fitness Centre, and set about making it a haven for the beautiful people of Mexia. With the oil bubble still dripping money over the Lone Star State, Stanford quickly found the cash-on-the-hip clientele he so desired, and Total Fitness Centres were seen as the crème de la crème of the gym world to the streams of new Texan yuppies.

According to several of the gym employees, Stanford was a regular at his own gym, liking nothing more than grunting loudly as he pumped iron or slamming the weights down for all to see whenever he finished a few reps. To everyone else who paid their gym fees, the latter of these peacock-esque displays of arrogance were strictly off-limits. Still, as you will see throughout this book, Robert (sorry, Allen) Stanford was a man who thrived on letting people know that rules did not apply to him.

With the early eighties kicking into gear, it is very easy to imagine the big Texan with his sweat-covered bronzed skin, huge obnoxious moustache, loud booming voice, and arrogant air as he marched through his own fitness centres wearing a half-length T-shirt and tiny Adidas shorts. Of course, we can only speculate, but by all accounts of Stanford around this time, he carried on in a way the Coen brothers would struggle to emulate on the silver screen.

Around this time, Stanford was known to land his helicopter in the car park of his gyms. Even in a state where brash, showy behaviour is not only tolerated but encouraged, Stanford's arrogant shows of wealth were seen as tactless. This was at a time when he only had three fitness centres, so arriving to work in a chopper would have been considered just a little over the top.

Stanford soon opened several more fitness centres around Texas, with each one rapidly becoming a gold mine. Of course, in the mid-seventies, the oil bubble was still expanding to an unimaginable size, and anyone with two cents to rub together could throw them up in the air and catch five dollars when it came back down.

Despite the massive profits he was making through his fitness centre empire, Stanford felt he was spending an awful lot of money on gym equipment. With this in mind, he decided to open up his own factory specialising in the manufacturing of dumbbells, weight benches, rowing machines, and whatever else he needed to stock his gyms.

How much of the equipment he had to replace after he had slammed it to the floor in a show of strength is unknown, but this move only goes to show the sheer lengths he would go to have total control.

His high-end fitness centres continued to thrive. In the first of many moves that would later blow up in his face, he decided to spread his empire to the much wealthier—and therefore more appealing—neighbouring city of Houston. It seemed that monopolising the gym market in Austin, Galveston, and Mexia wasn't enough for the moustachioed Texan, and it was this need to be forever richer that would eventually see him in an orange jumpsuit.

As Stanford was in Houston, cutting the ribbon—with oversized scissors, I'm sure—on his largest and most lavish fitness centre yet, the oil bubble that had turned everyone in the South into a John D. Rockefeller burst. Almost overnight, the cost of a barrel of oil dropped from around $34 to just over $10, and many businesses began shutting their doors on a daily basis.

Stanford hadn't been involved in the oil business, but the fallout of the market crashing affected everyone. As a new depression ripped through the States, regular Joes and Janes suddenly had no disposable income. This meant extravagances such as relaxing or working out in their local fitness centres became impossible, and with the fall in readily available cash, Stanford saw his Total Fitness Centre chain begin to rattle.

With the amount of money he had pumped into his latest venture in Houston, Stanford was at a crossroads. Should he see out the depression and hope he still had enough capital to go again when the financial restraints on the public loosened? Or should he cut his losses and run? As you may have guessed, the latter would always be more appealing to a man like Allen Stanford!

As everyone around him lost their jobs and houses, Stanford acted fast. He sold all of his fitness centres and reinvested the money in real estate, snapping up the homes and businesses of those who had recently lost them. He also rented a 45-story building in Central Houston and established the Guardian Development Corporation (GDC). This would later become the Stanford Development Company (SDC), and the tradition of the owner naming everything he touched after himself would be truly born!

As soon as his company was established in Houston, Allen began purchasing property on the cheap in that area too. Around this time, he brought his father in as a partner and consultant. All of this coincided with the widely publicised bankruptcy of the Exxon Oil Company and the ensuing closure of their massive Lago refinery in Aruba. One of the largest oil companies in the world, Exxon, would have to pay out a whopping $160 million in severance pay to its workers, meaning a whole lot of money had been stuffed in the pockets of many who didn't understand how investment worked.

Smelling an opportunity, Stanford flew out to Aruba to meet with the suddenly cash-rich Lago workers. Having never seen such a large amount of money in their bank account before and completely oblivious when it came to real estate, Stanford began pitching his newly purchased Texan properties to them. Many people invested in GDC, and Stanford suddenly had more capital than he knew what to do with. Of course, it technically wasn't his money, but little issues like that were never something Allen worried about.

With so much investment sitting there and nothing worthwhile to invest it in, Stanford made the decision to move it all to an offshore bank. Now, he could have used one of many offshore banks existing at the time, but through his mistrust or, more likely, cunning plan to bleed the money into his pocket, he decided to open up his own one in Montserrat, a British Territory in the Caribbean. He named it the Guardian International Bank (GIB), and they were ready for business in the summer of 1985.

A year after opening GIB, the world-famous Shell Oil Company suffered the same fate as Exxon had a year before, only this time they had to pay out over $200 million. Their refinery was also based in the same area as Exxon's (a small island just shy of Aruba), and much like their neighbours, the ex-employees of Shell were flush. Stanford and his father employed the same tactic of flying over, wowing the newly (and extremely gullible) rich with a seminar on how they could multiply their windfall by investing with them and stuffing the poor unsuspecting sods like a Christmas turkey.

As the eighties started to draw to a close, the stain the burst oil bubble had left on the Texan economy began to fade. Property prices went up once again, and once Stanford's portfolio had been sold off, he had nothing much left for him in his place of birth. Buying more houses to flip was out of the question, given their rising market value, and even if he'd wanted to, things had gotten a little hot for Stanford in America. Besides, his offshore bank in Montserrat had become a thriving business, with over $150 million in loyal clientele's cash and assets to play with.

But we're getting ahead of ourselves, as we haven't even discussed the real reasons behind Stanford's decision to 'emigrate' to the Caribbean. Yes, he needed to go there to run his lavish offshore bank and bask in the glory that came with being Sir Allen Stanford, but to pretend like these were the only aspects of his move would be remiss of us. We haven't even gotten to the FBI, the Ponzi schemes, the $20 million cricket game, or any of the other wonderfully Stanford-ish dealings that sent him scampering over the United States border and into the welcoming arms of the Caribbean Islands.

Stanford and the Caribbean

After the collapse of the economy in the States, and especially in Texas, Allen Stanford and his fitness clubs were hit hard. With rumours of his shady dealings already reaching the authorities in America and Stanford filing for bankruptcy, things looked bleak. When he disappeared off the face of the Earth for a whole year, the people back home wondered what had become of the gym owner who liked to land his helicopter in the car parks of his gyms.

Given that Stanford had recently declared that his companies were broke, it might have come as a surprise to most when he resurfaced on the little British-owned Caribbean island of Montserrat a year later with cash on the hip. Of course, that news would have been dwarfed by the declaration that he planned on opening—of all things—a bank, especially with his recent financial track record.

In the mid-to-late seventies, offshore banks in Montserrat were a dime a dozen, and rumours abounded among the wealthy and the shady that opening one was as easy as growing a moustache. Around the time Allen was deciding to dip his toe into the banking game, the island only had a population of 10,000; yet, despite this relatively small population, there were a staggering 300-plus banks registered. The majority of the people who lived on Montserrat were considered to be on third-world salaries, so having that many banks on such a small space of land should have been a red flag to the FBI earlier than it was.

For Stanford and many other greedy opportunists, Montserrat was a goldmine—a place where a man could open an offshore bank with a fistful of dollars and start selling certificates of deposits (CDs) and racking up money on the same day. It is said that Stanford heard about the offshore banking trade from a wealthy client he had been teaching how to scuba dive a few years before, and once he had been informed that Montserrat was like the Wild West for bankers, Stanford was already sold.

Usually, with a CD, the person handing over their money understands that the company they're giving it to will invest it wisely, usually in real estate or stocks. Of course, these companies need to have the required paperwork to back up their claims, but given the type of clientele Stanford was initially dealing with, a paper trail would have been the last thing they wanted.

Within a year of having settled there, Stanford had opened the Guardian International Bank (GIB). With his father James beside him, they began searching for wealthy clients—mainly in Latin America—who they wooed into buying their CDs and other investment opportunities. Of course, GIB ran like a regular bank on the surface, but only to the wealthy. Most of their incoming cash came in the form of larger deposits, with the client being promised it would be invested elsewhere with a guarantee of a 2-3% return for their money.

Now, where Stanford's bank differed from all of the other questionable offshore banks was that the returns they promised actually seemed feasible. Where past Ponzi schemes offered preposterous returns such as 20 or even 30%, GIB's lower offer was probably the deciding factor in a lot of clients handing over their money. It was this perfectly realistic return that would have resulted in the clientele's guard being let down before the killer blow was inflicted on their unsuspecting pockets.

Another aspect that made GIB stand out was Stanford actually went to the effort of commissioning the construction of a brick-and-mortar building. At a time when most—if not all—of the banks in the Caribbean were simply a brass plaque on a wall, being able to physically step into a bank and deal with people was a huge selling point and set Stanford's operation apart.

Of course, the actual bank itself was just a ruse. Some stories from the employees at the time have spoken of computers that weren't even plugged in, an office door leading to an empty room, and the rest of the building being nothing but a disused supermarket. Most of these rumours have been retold and recycled over the years, but even if Stanford's bank was just the shell it was told to be, it was still more than the rest of the competition.

The building itself was a gimmick, a background for him to snap photos of smiling secretaries and big business handshakes he could put on the cover of their fancy brochures. Much like the man himself, the shell of the place was completely different from what people really got inside, but it all worked for him nonetheless. He even created a backstory, claiming the bank had been run for generations and it was 75 years old. Of course, he did all this to give it a rich history and character and, in turn, gain the trust of potential clients.

Stanford's bank quickly took off, and soon he needed to expand his new empire. To do this, he moved some of his business over to the 45-story building he had previously purchased in Central Houston, where he had established the Guardian Development Corporation. Now, he was able to spread the weight of the overwhelming number of clients that were starting to come over to Guardian International Bank between his offices in the Caribbean and Houston.

But he needed more people on the board of directors he could trust, and 14 years after he walked out of Baylor University with a BA in finance, Stanford put a call in to his old friend and former college roommate, Alan Davis. The man who would become the AC to Stanford's DC had already built up quite an impressive career himself, but the lure of working alongside someone he'd always idolised was seemingly too much to resist.

In 1988, Davis uprooted his family from their home in Kalamazoo, Michigan and moved them out to Houston, where he was set to take a management role at GDC. This was now essentially a sister company for Stanford's bank on Montserrat, and it handled any overflow the GIB couldn't manage. Davis worked there for a year, in what Stanford would later say was a trial period to test his loyalty, before he was asked to pack his and his family's things up once more.

This time, Stanford flew them out to the Caribbean, where his old chum could join him at the main table. Nepotism was something Stanford lived by, and filling the board of directors with family and friends became his modus operandi. Having employees who only say 'yes' can be good for stroking one's ego, but it can also be a disastrous business approach, as Allen would find out years later.

As the eighties turned into the nineties, Stanford had well and truly made his mark on the Caribbean. For anyone who visited the tiny island of Montserrat at the time, they would have been greeted by a place that was Stanford-influenced from top to bottom. There was, of course, his grotesquely oversized stately home on the coast, with its marbled floors, fountains, and ostentatious yacht, which he kept close by at all times. Apart from his residence, there was the main cricket ground he had named after himself, several Stanford-owned restaurants, his athletics club, his local newspaper offices, and even two Stanford-themed domestic airlines that operated on the island.

But it's easy for us to paint Stanford as a mouthy, over-the-top cardboard cut-out of a man, swanning around his little island and tossing silver dollars to the locals, as there genuinely is a hint of that to him. But to the people who lived there, Allen Stanford was —and in some cases, still is—loved for his generosity. Not just that, but the buildings he commissioned were done to the highest standard, and the majority of them are still in use today, albeit for less crooked dealings!

He offered wage packets to his employees that had been unseen on Montserrat before his arrival, with the waiters in his restaurants earning more than the local government officials. They got quarterly bonuses, benefits, and lavish staff parties. Stanford might have been bleeding his investors dry, but he was flashing their cash elsewhere.

By 1990, the bank was thriving. Alan Davis was on the island too, and things couldn't have been sweeter. Investors from Latin America seemed to be sending new money to be invested on a daily basis. Every new restaurant or athletics club on the island felt like it was Stanford built—and they usually were—and the man himself had been seen more than once in a director's box at the cricket matches.

But behind the scenes, everything wasn't as it seemed, though. The whole world of offshore banking had come to the attention of law enforcement, and the Wild West reputation of the Caribbean Islands—especially Montserrat—had become too much to ignore. Word of dirty money and shady dealings were filtering down to the men and women on the street back in the States, and in the late eighties, the FBI and Scotland Yard met in secret to discuss an international collaborative task force to investigate the activities.

It was formed quickly, with their only goal to work side by side to bring down the crooked bankers on the Caribbean Islands and the surrounding areas. Many rich men soon started to fall, and the greedier ones—those who offered 20-30% returns—were the first to go. Stanford initially flew under the radar, as his promised 2-3% seemed pretty much above board. Also, he had built a brick-and-mortar building—not to mention the money he was pumping back into the island—so he would have been very low on the task force's list.

That soon changed, though, and when rumours of money laundering began to swirl around, Stanford and his Guardian International Bank couldn't operate in the shadows anymore. And they weren't (supposedly) money laundering for just anyone. No, if the stories are to be believed, and we have no reason to see them as false, much of the incoming cash the GIB saw was from Colombia and, to be a bit more specific, the Medellin and Cali drug cartels.

In the late seventies, the cartels in Colombia had started covering America and, later, Europe in a cloud of white powder. By the eighties, cocaine was the drug of choice for everyone, from the guy who worked in the local garage to the doctors and politicians they trusted. The profits made from shipping and selling the drug were astronomical, but there was one downside—transactions were always made in cash.

The cartels needed ways to make the large sums of physical money become legal tender, so they often turned to crooked banks. Once they handed their money over, these banks would filter it back into the system through certificates of deposits, dodgy investments, real estate, and any number of apparently legitimate avenues. The likes of Pablo Escobar—who was heavily linked to Stanford at the time—would lose a chunk of their money in the filtering process, but it would come out clean in the end, which was priceless to them.

Meanwhile, Alan Davis, the once reserved and calm young man from Texas, was gradually becoming more and more like his idol. He divorced his first wife, Ruth, with whom he had two young sons, and began a relationship with their 16-year-old babysitter, Lori. The breakup and the embarrassing nature of it was too much to bear for Ruth, and she took her own life not long after, stepping in front of an oncoming truck.

In her will, she left her grand estate—she had been awarded it in the divorce—to her two sons, Zack and Will, who were seven and five, respectively. Unfortunately, the will itself wasn't watertight, and Davis and his lawyers were able to successfully turn the whole thing over to him. He quickly sold it and purchased a new 50-foot yacht which he kept moored in a marina off Miami, where he spent many cosy evenings aboard with his new bride and former babysitter.

Throughout the late eighties and early nineties, Davis' love of vanity surgeries had really taken hold, and he spent millions on face lifts, tummy tucks, and several penis enlargements. It seemed he was willing to go to unimaginable lengths to become a big, brash dick-swinging banker like his buddy, Allen.

During one of his many plastic surgery exploits, Davis had a bad reaction to the anaesthesia, and he was hospitalised for a significant amount of time. He had flown back to Houston for the operation, and while he was gone, things back on Montserrat took a turn for the worse too.

In 1991, Allen Stanford and his GIB had their banking licence revoked due to suspicious activity and failure to meet specific criteria. The bank's assets were frozen, and the task force that had been set up a few years previously began to close in. Unlike some of the other offshore bankers, Stanford proved more slippery, and they struggled to make much of what they wanted to pin on him to actually stick for any length of time.

A lot of Stanford's protection came from the Montserrat authorities and government officials, who were clearly in his pocket. Of course, nearly two decades later, when Stanford was finally arrested, these people denied any links whatsoever. Given how many permits Stanford received no-questions-asked, and the endless number of blind eyes turned, we have to assume he was getting some form of special treatment.

Still, the noose was tightening nonetheless, and much like his time in Texas when things went south (pun most definitely intended), Stanford was left with two choices: stay where he was and fight the accusations legally and fairly, or tuck tail and run.

Being an honourable man, he chose to stay and fight his case... No, sorry, of course he didn't!

Stanford instantly sent his people to the surrounding islands to find a place as suitable as Montserrat had been. He quickly found one that was even better, as it had recently become independent from Britain, and their laws—specifically those concerned with banking—were completely up in the air. Stanford and his board of directors caught them all on the way back down and rearranged them to suit their agenda.

The place they chose to set up their new bank was Antigua, a beautiful island only 17 miles from Montserrat. At the time, the island's economy desperately needed investment, and it was in severe financial dire straits, so much so that the largest bank on the island, the Bank of Antigua (BOA), was on the verge of foreclosure. It seemed all of the pieces had fallen into place for Stanford once again, and after getting a letter of good standing from the Minister of Finance on Montserrat, he officially moved his operations over to Antigua and purchased the BOA's building. Clearly not a fan of irony, Stanford told his employees the relocation was all legit and that Montserrat's banking system had become far too lawless for him!

In late 1990 and early 1991, Stanford began snapping up property all over the island. As he had done in Montserrat, and to a lesser extent, Texas, he became like an overgrown child playing Monopoly, who believes if he buys every square he lands on, there is no way he can lose. Of course, life—and even the world-famous board game—doesn't work that way, as the person flashing the cash quickly has no money left to maintain the endless businesses and property they've acquired. Any money they need to pay for future goods and services is nonexistent, and the whole infrastructure crumbles from the inside out.

Stanford didn't think in those terms, and to him, money was never an issue. If he needed more, he just hooked another wealthy sucker to 'invest' in GIB or his real estate portfolio. To the people who gave him their cash and life savings, in some cases, they genuinely thought they were setting themselves up for a financially secure retirement.

One of Stanford's shrewder traits was that he knew how to plug into the desires of regular folks and build their excitement and thus their loyalty. He pumped money into local sports, never shy of showing up with his 24/7 camera crew in tow to pose for pictures with the kids as they smiled and thanked the giant Texan for making their dreams come true. He bought restaurants and hired the town's residents to work there, giving them substantial pay packets and bonuses.

And he saw that in the Caribbean, one sport reigned over all others. To some, it was almost a religion, something that, when they played it, they could compete with those nations that had recently oppressed them. It was an equaliser that could be experienced by everyone who wanted to play. On the Caribbean Islands and the West Indies, bowling and batting were just a way of life.

Of course, we are talking about cricket, and Stanford would have known that if he held their favourite sport up on a silver platter and dressed it in chopped parsley and foie gras, the people of Antigua would love him. He would become untouchable, and most of all, he would be idolised.

There was one holdup, though. Stanford was from the land of Super Bowls, World Series, and Stanley Cups. He liked quick-fire action and Ws at the buzzer. Sport should be all-action and glamour, not long breaks and crumpets. It didn't matter to him that cricket had centuries of history behind it and certain rules and codes of ethics that needed to be abided to. Allen Stanford was someone who made his own rules, and as we've seen from his fabricated tales of 75-year-old banks and Hollywood-type exploits on the college football field, he also created his own history when needed.

Cricket would bend to his will if he threw enough money at it, he knew. Why wouldn't it, when everything else he'd ever doused in cash had always learned to heel? If Stanford could bring cricket to where he wanted it to be, then the people of Antigua would not only love him, they might just see him as a god!

Caribbean Cricket's Soul for Sale

Cricket in Antigua has always been undoubtedly the most popular sport on the island. In fact, as we've discussed, it is like a religion to most people in the West Indies. By the time Stanford moved 17 miles northeast of Montserrat to snap up the Bank of Antigua in the mid-90s, West Indian cricket was at an all-time low.

Amazingly, this slump had come after the most dominant period in the history of test cricket, when the Windies went unbeaten for a staggering 15 years between 1980 and 1995. Their mixture of fast bowling and flamboyant batting had never been seen before, and they seemed to break new ground with every test match. Legendary players like Sir Viv Richards, Malcolm Marshall, Desmond Haynes, and at the tail-end of the run, the great Brian Lara swept the world of cricket aside. It was a period of dominance that had never been seen and will realistically never be equalled.

But directly after the run ended, West Indies cricket suffered an unimaginable slump. Even during the Golden Age, rumours always abounded of a lack of funding, low pay for players, and corruption in high places. The bubble seemed forever in danger of bursting, and when it did, the reality was that cricket in the Windies—most prominently in the smaller islands—was in trouble.

When a big, loud Texan arrived with his pockets bulging and a glint in his eye, there were sceptics among the Antiguans. Rich

Westerners settling on the islands and buying up local businesses wasn't unheard of, so Allen Stanford's arrival was seen as just another mogul who preferred to run things a little differently than his homeland and its laws expected.

Stanford's involvement in cricket is a strange one at best. For those who sat with him at games or chatted about the sport at his ostentatious mansion, he is recalled as being utterly clueless as to what it all meant. Later, as he started to come into the cricket world's consciousness through his Stanford 20/20 tournament and, of course, his landing of a helicopter at Lord's, it is clear he polished up on the basics for appearances. He knew the buzz words, the lingo, and the basics, but it was all done to paint over the cracks of reality.

We may be able to see through the whole charade today by simply watching a YouTube video of him prattling on about cricket needing to be more like the OK Corral or mincing around the stadium ogling the player's wives, but hindsight is a wonderful thing. At the time—both in the West Indies and later in England—Stanford pounced on an opportunity. Each time the Windies and the English were in dire straits financially, and the sight of piles of money would have been hard to resist, more so when it was dangled with the promise of more to come.

Stanford was a shark when it came to money worries in others, and when he smelt their fear in the water, he was quick to react. Ironically in life, those who are struggling financially are often the very people who roll the dice on whatever chunk of it they have left. Stanford always abided by this tactic, which is why he targeted a sport that was so dear to people's hearts but also in trouble and in need of a saviour. It's also why he set his sights on the elderly in his Ponzi schemes, as he preyed on their dreams of a cosy retirement by promising guaranteed returns on their investments.

Long before the first Stanford 20/20 tournament, the man himself went to work on other aspects of monopolising Antigua. Again, it must be mentioned that for those who lived in relative poverty on the island before his arrival, many still speak highly of all he did there. Much like Montserrat, Stanford pumped a hell of a lot of money into malls, restaurants and, of course, cricket pitches and stadiums. At the time of his arrest, he employed more people on the island than anyone else.

But before all of that, when he got the whiff of West Indian cricket's desperation, they were at their lowest ebb. Before the late nineties, the terrible pay the players received and the awful conditions they trained on could almost be ignored because results on the pitch were so impeccable. The players were treated like gods, at least in terms of respect among the locals, and probably had no idea of the money being made in other countries. Back when sportspeople represented their nation for pride and not a new Bugatti with a flamingo feather interior, the privilege of stepping onto that field was often rewarding enough, and the higher-ups were more than happy to pay them in plaudits instead of cash.

Early on in his move into cricket, most of the legends of the West Indies game were sceptical of what Allen Stanford represented. Michael Holding—whose wife would later work for Stanford through her management company—spoke of one incident in particular when he was watching a game with the Texan.

According to Whispering Death, as Holding was known through his exploits as a Jamaican cricket god, he sat beside Stanford at one of his early 20/20 games. When Allen saw the fast bowlers scuffing the turf with their studs to mark their run-up, he was furious. He ranted to Holding about how disgraceful it was that they were messing up his pitch and declared that they should use AstroTurf instead, as it would look better and not get marked.

Stanford was more concerned with aesthetics and how "his pitch" would appear on camera. This sort of reaction is indicative of the man and his time in cricket, and he wanted everything to be bigger, bolder, faster, and more entertaining. Seemingly, it never entered his mind that millions of people had found the sport— specifically the lengthy test cricket he dismissed so readily— entertaining already. It takes a certain type of neurotic narcissist to constantly remain utterly oblivious to everyone else's opinion, but Stanford had that particular trait in spades.

When rumblings of Stanford's plan to expand 20/20 in the West Indies really began to catch fire, the public was split. On the one hand, they were test cricket people, enamoured with the beauty of long, drawn-out matches. On the flip side, they saw real potential in the financial gain of bowing to Stanford's will. As we've discussed already, Stanford had a way of getting people excited, and the storm he whipped up regarding where he could take Windies cricket was no different in that regard.

Maybe as a sign of goodwill, or just to get his fingers in as many pies as possible, Stanford handed out around $250,000 each to at least 20 of the islands for them to pump into their grassroots cricket. He built training facilities and state-of-the-art pitches and hired nutritionists to help the players reach their ultimate potential. His determination and loyalty to the game seemed genuine, and even some of the legends of the sport who had questioned his motives early on began to come over to his side.

Stanford filled his cricket board with the holiest of ex-batsmen and bowlers. Soon he had the likes of the aforementioned Michael Holding and Sir Viv Richards sitting around the table. They were joined by Sir Everton Weekes, Sir Garfield Sobers, Lance Gibbs, and Curtly Ambrose, among others. Stanford was stacking the deck, and much like his business model of buying up everything in sight and dealing with the consequences later, he clearly believed cricket could be overwhelmed in the same manner.

By the early 2000s, the Stanford 20/20 tournament was starting to look like a reality. No longer a funny joke among the locals, real strides were being made to bring it all together, and the rest of the cricket world was starting to lift their heads ever so slightly above the tall grass and take a peek. Stadiums were being renovated and even built from scratch to accommodate the competition to come. In the 90s, Stanford had set up cricketing schools for the youngsters, and as the first 20/20 in 2006 approached, some of those who had come through the academies were starting to make waves in the under 19s and 21s teams.

Laurie-Ann Holding, a successful businesswoman and wife of Michael Holding, had been introduced to Stanford a few years before the start of his 20/20 shenanigans. After witnessing a party her company threw for a fellow wannabe aristocrat, he hired her to do the same for his tournament. She and her company's job would be to promote the upcoming event, play host to the investors and big shots, and look after festivities when the actual games began.

Years later, she would speak of the extravagances Stanford demanded, including the lengths he was willing to go to for promotion. He wanted adverts on every TV channel on all of the islands, and he wanted them running almost continuously. When informed of the sheer cost of such an endeavour, he is said to have dismissed such issues as folly. Again, he wanted bigger, bolder, and better, which included an outlandish request to get David Beckham and Rihanna to come over and film ads for his tournament.

Unfortunately, the Beckham and Rihanna idea never came to fruition, which is a shame, as seeing Becks claiming Babe Ruth to be his all-time favourite cricket player would have been priceless.

But joking aside, Stanford meant business, and he instantly handed Laurie-Ann's company a cool $20 million to splash on the promotion of the 2006 Stanford 20/20.

Cardigan Connor, the former Antiguan-born English cricketer, was managing a team on one of the smaller islands, Anguilla, at the time of Stanford's cricket adventure. Like many others, he had come around to the idea, but merely because he had already seen the fruits of the financial investment at a grassroots level. He found that kids were now viewing cricket as a legitimate career choice and not a pastime, simply because now, they could make a living from playing the sport they loved.

Lester Bird, the 2nd Prime Minister of Antigua and Barbuda from 1994 to 2004, spoke highly of Stanford at the time of the Texan's residence there. Of course, by 2009, he had changed his tune like so many others who had been part of Stanford's dealings, but he still admitted that many of the hospitals and new roads wouldn't have been on the island if it wasn't for his one-time moustachioed pal.

With Bird being a massive cricket fan, he was more than happy with what was being done for the sport in the West Indies, and despite everything we know about Stanford today, the excitement at the time was genuine, and rightly so. Lester Bird would have had a front-row seat to the positive changes occurring across the islands, and any fears people had about how the Stanford 20/20 would go down soon changed their minds when the first games were roaring successes, both in entertainment and coverage.

The Bird family's time in politics would be fraught with controversy and rumours of gun-smuggling and kickbacks, so their connection to Stanford would probably have been expected. Still, dirty money is sometimes all a nation has, and when it is being used to build medical facilities, then the whole thing becomes a bit of a double-edged sword.

One of the major roadblocks for Allen Stanford was his insistence on shorter, punchier games. As we've covered already, test cricket and the whole process involved had been around for over a century, and for those who played the sport, it was the only way. The bright-coloured kits, big lights, and fast action seemed to be far too Americanised, and for the connoisseur of cricket, the game's soul was being sold.

The Stanford 20/20 was more concerned with glamour than history and TV ratings over substance. It was modernised in a way that seemed the polar opposite of everything cricket stood for, and for many, it was hard to watch. It must have seemed like a loved one being slowly strangled by a spangle-covered foam finger.

Still, Stanford was adamant it would work, and as the tournament finally began, the general population fell in love very quickly. The 2006 Stanford 20/20 was held at the Stanford Cricket Ground (of course), in St John's, Antigua and Barbuda, to widespread acclaim. The rules, a slightly tweaked version of the English Twenty20 format, didn't ruffle as many feathers as first feared, and the advertising pre-tournament had worked a treat. TV figures were astronomically higher than forecasted, and the standard of play was incredible, adding up to what seemed like a perfect result for all involved.

The inaugural winners were Guyana, beating Trinidad and Tobago in the final in a closely contested, frantic affair that would have had the recently inaugurated Sir Allen beaming. Trinidad would go on to lift the sophomore—and last—Stanford 20/20 two years later, overcoming the mighty Jamaica at the Stanford Cricket Ground.

One thing that did happen and might have actually bettered seeing a bewildered David Beckham bumbling his way through an advert, was Stanford coming onto the pitch before the opening game to "throw the first ball". The idea is so "World Series" that it's almost impossible to imagine, but unfortunately, since no known coverage of it exists, using our imagination to picture it is all we can do!

The death of his 20/20 venture coincided with the FBI and Scotland Yard tightening the noose and upping the intensity of their investigations into his suspicious dealings, and the planned 2010 tournament never took place. It was also around the time when the man himself was landing a helicopter on the hallowed turf of Lord's with 20 million bucks in a Perspex case.

Even with the offshore banking task force sniffing around his dealings, Sir Allen was the type of man who seemed to want to step up his publicity instead of laying low. Had his arrogance gotten so out of control that he presumed himself untouchable? It's as perfectly feasible an answer as anyone is likely to find. He could have thought that hiding in plain sight negated his guilt because why on Earth would a man go on TV and pose for pictures in front of a colossal stack of cash unless he had nothing to hide?

Even before the 20/20 had begun, the task force had presumed his involvement in cricket was just another way for him to launder money. Rumours were still circulating that he had been dry cleaning cash for Pablo Escobar and the other cartels in Colombia—something Stanford vehemently denied—so using a sport as popular as cricket to launder his own money wouldn't have been so far-fetched.

Another theory—one suggesting the money he spent on cricket was genuine, at least in intention—is that he wanted to build the game up around himself to satisfy his God-complex. This hypothesis is as legitimate as any, as Stanford was known for constantly claiming he was the most popular man on the islands. He needed attention at all times—something that was proved by his 24/7 camera crew—and being in the limelight in the West Indies was a guarantee if you were the self-proclaimed saviour of cricket.

The money Stanford pumped into cricket might have reached its zenith between 2006 and 2008, but in truth, he had been helping the islands build the game for a lot longer. Whether he was just gaining their trust before he glamorised the sport with the first 20/20, we'll probably never know, but the fact remains that he made a lot of positive changes. It's easy for us to look back on that time and scowl at the islands' cricket boards and ask why they accepted what was clearly dirty money. Still, back then, nothing had been proven, and actually, unless you worked for the FBI or Scotland Yard, nothing had even been suspected, really.

Still, his main cricket board—the one adorned with some of the greatest names in West Indian cricket—began to lose some of its members over time, notably Michael Holding. He had grown weary of what he saw as the death of cricket as he'd known it and felt that hard, dusty pitches and low wages were better than full pockets and no soul. With his wife still working for Stanford, it probably made for some awkward Christmas parties, but Holding has always been known to his peers as an honest man, so we can assume he would not have stepped down from his position without legitimate concerns.

Summed up as much as humanly possible, Sir Allen Stanford's time in Caribbean cricket was, let's say... interesting.

There is no other way to put it, really, and much like his rumoured involvement in money laundering for Mr. Escobar and having umpteen illegitimate kids, a lot of what we know about him is coated in mystery and hearsay. It's easy to presume all of the good he did to be false and the bad to be true—and we can probably ascertain that this is closer to reality than not—but there is also clear evidence of some of the positives he did during his time on the islands.

Sure, much of the stuff he built was most certainly done with other people's money, and that pretty much discredits everything. But still, when it was happening at the time, those who witnessed it—including hundreds of thousands of West Indian cricket lovers—would have thought something magical was happening.

Sir Allen Stanford lived and breathed acclaim, and once he realised the power he could wield by controlling a sport that was so adored by the islands, he clamped his sparkplugs down on its beating heart and turned it up to overdrive. He loved being the man people fawned over, and more importantly, he knew how to make them do it.

But his time at the top wouldn't last, and not long after the last ball was thrown at a Stanford 20/20 game and the rotor blades of his sleek, black helicopter had stopped spinning on the Lord's Nursery Ground, everything as Sir Allen knew it came crashing down around him. But in classic Stanford style, he didn't go down without a fight, which could only mean one thing: entertainment of the highest calibre.

English Cricket's Reaction

"One night, one game, twenty million dollars!"

That was the claim of the loudmouthed Texan, Sir Allen Stanford, as he met the reporters and paparazzi at Lord's in June 2008. The pictures being beamed around the globe showed him standing beside ECB and World Cricket Board (WCB) bigwigs in front of a large Perspex box with a supposed $20 million in American bills. For the players on the English team, nothing like it had ever been seen before, and how they should react in an ethical sense—especially in the eyes of the public—was anyone's guess.

One train of thought was that they should just take the money and run, setting themselves up for life and getting back to real cricket when it was all done. Stanford's initial promise had been for his "one night, one game" match to be played once every year for five years, so it was suggested the players might as well suck it up and swallow their pride for the few hours it took to play the match. This particular view was generally taken by those who didn't want the British players jumping ship, so the very apparent shame in taking part could be overlooked by some fans if it kept the cream of the home-grown talent from moving to the recently formed—and very lucrative—Indian Premier League.

The English Twenty20, which had formed several years before Stanford's monstrosity, couldn't compete financially with the IPL. Their only bargaining chip to keep the English players from moving overseas was the threat of expulsion from any further test matches, and amazingly, it worked. In a time before the Millennial generation, playing on people's loyalties actually worked—as the average person had morals—and just about every British player decided against hopping on a plane to New Delhi and cashing in.

But the IPL was built by cricket people for cricket lovers, so it was nothing like Stanford's glitzy cricket Frankenstein creation in terms of what its goals were. India was a major force in the game, and even with the ECB staunchly against any of their players joining, it was at least seen as legitimate competition. Over time, more and more British players would make the change, but this only coincided with slight relaxations in the ECB's restrictions and the IPL's rearranging of fixture dates to avoid clashes with test matches.

The ECB's disdain of the IPL and the money it offered seemed all the more hypocritical that day in 2008 when the board members raced out to meet Stanford off his shiny helicopter on the Nursery Grounds at Lord's. After spending the previous year pelting as much stigma as they could at the IPL and voicing their concerns over the evils of cashing in on cricket, it might have irritated the British players who had chosen to stay on home soil just a little bit when they saw that Perspex box. In fact, it would probably have been the deciding factor for many in taking Stanford's offer at all, as their so-called leaders had bent the knee so readily.

Kevin Pietersen, England's captain at the time, was weary of Stanford from the moment they met. On Sir Allen's first appearance at an English cricket match, the Texan decided to waltz into the changing room before the game and bustle around from player to player, making as much of a scene as possible. It showed his complete lack of knowledge concerning the sport on British soil, as the player's changing room was off-limits to everyone but the players themselves and the coaching staff.

Stanford may have claimed ignorance when questioned on his

behaviour, but the reality is he would have been fully aware of what he was doing. Much like everything else in his life, he believed if he had thrown enough cash at something, it belonged to him, both in physical form and in soul. It is the classic narcissism we endlessly associate with him, and his need to dominate and fully consume all he owned (or believed he owned) would never be satisfied. In fact, for people like Stanford, the craving for complete and utter control only ever gets stronger.

Pietersen may have been suspicious of Sir Allen, but he still posed for pictures with the Stanford 20/20 trophy in the build-up to the match. On top of that, he signed a $500,000 contract with the Texan to be one of his ambassadors. He would never see the money and, in the end, claimed he actually made a financial loss due to the whole fiasco.

Speaking in February of 2009, Pietersen said, "I was an ambassador for Stanford, a player face, but that contract is gone".

"Stanford was a sleazebag. I was very uncomfortable with the whole thing. It was tacky. The public perception was that the England team had simply been sold to a bloke with a lot of money" (Hayter, 2009).

Despite Pietersen's admitted discomfort with the $20 million game, he continued to promote it on TV and in interviews. He may have done so with a forced smile, but for those who played along —which was basically everyone who stood to benefit—the damage to their integrity had already been done. Pietersen will be forever known as an English cricketing legend, though, and one silly mistake would never change that. Still, for him and everyone else around the game at the time, the bad taste the whole experience left in their mouths would always remain.

In the lead-up—and especially in the aftermath—of the game, the majority of scrutiny fell on the shoulders of the ECB, and rightly so. David Collier, in particular, was accused of ignoring all of the signs that something wasn't quite right, and it was suspected he had known all along what the risks might be, despite his endless denial. Even before the game, the heat had been turned up on Collier, and when Stanford's past dealings came to light months later, it would take more than an embroidered Lord's napkin to wipe the egg off his face.

The Professional Cricketers' Association (PCA) are said to have warned Collier and his cash-blinded cronies of the dangers involved. When the first news of Stanford's interest in such a bizarre cricket venture began circulating, the PCA told Collier directly not to get involved, but their warnings were ignored.

"We advised extreme caution over any dealings with Stanford," a PCA official claimed not long after everything went kaput. "There had been real danger signs coming out of the US for a long time, and the ECB should have seen them" (Hayter, 2009).

Fair warning, wouldn't you say? But money really does talk, even when the majority of it is just stuffed in a Perspex box.

The pressure on Collier didn't last, and he continued in his role up until 2014, even receiving his Order of the British Empire (OBE) a year later. It seemed by the time the Stanford storm had died down a little, everyone involved—and even those who weren't directly involved—just wanted it to be forgotten, especially Collier himself. It was the easier thing to do, but the fact remains that the man whose job it was to steer the cricket ship to greener pastures aimed it directly at a huge stack of money and sank it in a sea of humiliation.

The sport itself would rise again, and pretty quickly at that. Much like football teams who lose a Big-Time Charlie player to

Barcelona or Real Madrid, the game itself is bigger than any one person, even men like Collier or Giles Clarke. Whether they ever knew the full extent of Stanford's shady character when they signed cricket's soul over to him, we'll never know, but we have to suppose at least some of the stench got through the mouth-watering odour of American bills.

Ed Joyce and Tim Murtagh, two Irish cricketers playing for Middlesex at the time, were flown over to Antigua before the big game to participate in a couple of warm-up friendlies with the England team. Under the low lights (we'll get into that later), with black bats in hand (again, we'll get there) and silver stumps (ditto), the Middlesex players stepped out for a single game worth $280,000.

Now, that seems like nothing compared to the cool $20 million on the main game to come a few weeks later, but it was still a handy payday for whatever team won. Trinidad and Tobago, the recent winners of the 2008 Stanford 20/20, tagged along too and played a separate match against the English in front of a packed Stanford Cricket Ground. It was all a bit glitzy and over the top, but we're talking about Sir Allen Stanford here, so nothing less would have done.

Still, the idea of playing under such circumstances hadn't been viewed as it is today. As we are discovering throughout this story, hindsight will always play a massive part in the whole thing. Maybe the players saw it as a bit of a laugh? A quick way to make a few quid and have a little fun while they were there. For some, it was a free trip to beautiful Antigua, and if the man paying for everything wanted them to use black bats while they played, then so be it.

Speaking about that night under the terrible lighting, Ed Joyce said, "It didn't seem strange at all. This super-wealthy guy thought it was a good idea so we didn't question it at all. Not many people would have known who Allen Stanford was at the time, so it just wasn't a big deal" (Johns, 2022).

And that was the view of a lot of the players: What did it matter if this tanned, charismatic Texan wanted to "put on a show"? It was still cricket, after all, if a little glitzy and fake, but cricketers were working stiffs too, and the idea of making some extra pocket change while experiencing a new culture would be tempting to anyone.

And that holiday aspect came into play quite often, as Joyce mentioned in the same interview. "Myself and the wife got married just before it, and we were supposed to go on our honeymoon straight after the summer to Argentina. We ended up going to Antigua instead" (Johns, 2022).

Flashy kits and poor lighting aside, the rest of the mini-tour had been organised very professionally. All of the players who took part spoke very highly of what they had been greeted with, and the narrative that everything Stanford built was nothing more than a cardboard background that looked good on camera but fell over close up couldn't have been further from the truth. There were issues with lighting and other minor details, but all-in-all, it was seen as a pretty decent setup.

Joyce's teammate, fellow Irishman and Middlesex star Tim Murtagh confirmed how most players felt.

"To be fair, the whole thing was really well run. People picked us up from the airport, they all had the Stanford clothing with the logos on, and the buses had Middlesex plastered on the side; it was all professionally done. We stayed at an all-inclusive resort called Jolly Beach. The ground itself was picturesque and had grassy banks all around it. Although the facilities were a bit ropey" (Johns, 2022).

So it seemed much of what had been set up by Stanford looked okay at first glance, but as was usually the case with Sir Allen's ventures, the core of what he was selling was rotten. Everyone was there to dance to his tune like organ grinders' monkeys, and the cricket was just the pre-entertainment before the actual Stanford Show. A lot of the players felt used, and rightly so, as they had become nothing but actors in a big, blown-up matinee of glitter and cash and all things moustache.

Never one to mince his words, English cricket legend and bona fide just-one-of-the-guys Freddie Flintoff was outspoken about Stanford early on. In one of his plethora of autobiographies, he tore into Sir Allen and everything surrounding the England versus Stanford Superstars game.

"I had reservations about the England team's association with Allen Stanford even before we flew out to Antigua for the first of our Twenty20 challenge matches and they were just compounded once we arrived.

"All the talk about England helping the development of West Indies cricket was absolute rubbish. We should have come out and said that we were there as mercenaries, playing for money. It was nothing to do with playing for England or helping Caribbean cricket" (Ishmael, 2009).

Harsh words, but again, they were spoken after the game took place. Many people since have asked why none of the players had decided against the game at the time, but as the representatives of the PCA later claimed, David Collier and the ECB apparently put heavy pressure on them to sign up to Allen Stanford's deal. Of course, the thoughts of winning a million dollars per man might have swayed them either way, but still, it can't have been a pleasant situation to have been put in.

Flintoff aimed some of the blame at himself and the players too, though. He claimed there was a belief floating around that they could fly out to the West Indies a week before the game, play a couple of warm-up friendlies, and be ready for the main $20 million game against a team who had been training for six weeks.

Still, this sort of admission only refers to the match's result and not the large amount of money on offer for the winners. But regardless of everything else that went down, Flintoff seemed most upset at being moved around like a giant pawn for a man who believed he could—and essentially did—buy anyone he wanted.

"I was uncomfortable being a plaything for an American businessman," Flintoff went on to say in his 19th or 20th autobiography that year. "The cricket was a sideshow, and we were just puppets. The trip didn't seem to be popular with anyone, not in the dressing room, and most of the publicity was negative" (Flintoff, 2009).

We'll never know how the English players would have felt about the whole thing if they'd won and flown home with a million quid each instead of just their tails between their legs, as the one and only game against the Stanford Superstars was a demolition job which the Windies won easily. I'm sure every single English player would claim the money wasn't important and that they had been forced into it, and there is probably some truth to that, but an extra million in the bank can sure take the sting out of feeling dejected.

The general consensus will always be that English cricket and the ECB sold their souls to a loud Texan with an even louder

48

moustache. But we need to remember that despite the brightly coloured uniforms and inappropriate touching of players' wives, Sir Allen had done some wonderful things for West Indies cricket, at least financially. It is easy to assume the money was all the ECB saw, and it surely was the deciding factor, but there were other variables too.

As we've discussed, the birth of the Indian Premier League had gone better than anyone could have expected, and the temptation for Britain's best players seemed as though it would only get harder to resist. If the ECB were approaching the whole thing as a means to an end, it could be slightly easier to forgive. Much like the wealthy, obnoxious, overbearing uncle who shows up to your house every Christmas in your youth, tolerating his nonsense for an hour might just result in a £20 note being slipped into your hand as he leaves, so grinning and bearing it can seem like the lesser of two evils.

Maybe the plan was to tolerate Stanford for a week or two a year, get the players some big money, and in turn, make the IPL a less attractive option? Or perhaps the ECB simply saw dollar signs and concluded their own pockets would get a hell of a lot fatter whether the England team won the match or not.

Whatever the case may be, the public was outraged. With one of the worst recessions in recent memory ripping through the world, the idea of some already well-paid—in terms of the men and women on the street—athletes getting a million dollars a man for one night's work looked terrible. Then there were the die-hard cricket fans, who saw the money only as a nail in the coffin of the sport they held so dear, and the slow, disappointed shaking of heads could be seen for miles.

The England team had worked so hard to leave the on-field disaster of the nineties behind, and the noughties had seen a steady rise in quality. All that effort was in danger of being undone in one night, and for those who had stood behind them during the slump of the previous decade, the Stanford Superstars game must have felt like a swift kick in the stumps.

Even as the dust settled and the players prepared their I-never-wanted-anything-to-do-with-it speeches, many if not all of them were thinking about the return fixture the following year. As good ol' Freddie Flintoff said in one of his autobiographies, the players were thinking more about better preparation next time round more so than the indignity of it all.

"The general feeling was that we would just turn up and win, collect the money, and go home. I thought that was unbelievable. Whoever put that itinerary together wasn't living in the real world. By the time we left Antigua, I think we were united in our determination to do things differently the next time, should there be one. A few months later, Stanford's business empire collapsed, so that trip was the first and last of its kind" (Flintoff, 2009).

Robbing Peter to Pay Paul: The Birth(ish) of the Ponzi Scheme

Before Allen Stanford, and even before Bernard Madoff (a $65 billion rip-off, thank you very much!), there was Charles Ponzi. The man who the Ponzi scheme was named after wasn't actually the first to think up a scam offering ridiculous returns on people's investments with no intention of ever giving them their money, but he was certainly the first to do it on such a massive scale.

Now, you might be wondering why we are talking about Charles Ponzi in a book about Allen Stanford's life and cricket, but it is pretty essential if we're to understand how the minds of such hucksters work. We will cover the basics of Ponzi schemes and how the general public can fall into the traps that seem so obvious in the aftermath. Also, the things Charles Ponzi got up to were fantastically entertaining, so it will be well worth your while!

The general trend is that most con artists such as Ponzi and Stanford often seem to be born and raised in lower-to-middle class families. Another commonality in the makeup of these guys is that they are usually raised in a family that, at one stage or another, was rather more wealthy. By the time these little Allens and Charles' are chomping on Rusks or pulling their first grift in playschool, only the memory of their family's status remains. We can suppose it was this feeling of missing out on the lavish life they presumed to be rightfully theirs that led to such delusions of grandeur, but whatever the reasons behind who they became, all of them were sociopaths and egomaniacs through either nature or nurture.

There is no other way for such a person to be built if they are to grow up and steal from thousands of people, and Charles Ponzi was no different.

Born in Lugo, Raveena, Italy, on 3 March 1882 to a poor yet once-wealthy family, little (take a breath before you say it) Carlo Pietro Giovanni Guglielmo Tebaldo Ponzi grew up believing he deserved something more. Even though his family were desperately poor, his mother still used the title 'Donna', proving the delusions of grandeur that drove him were genetically inherent.

Carlo held down a couple of menial jobs in his youth, most notably as a postal worker, and somehow managed to secure himself a place at the University of Rome after he left school. Instead of seizing this opportunity to better himself educationally, Ponzi is said to have spent his four years there pulling minor swindles and partaking in petty gambling. This need to get rich quickly would always be a part of his life, and like most schemers and con artists, their belief that they deserve to be on top must only be achieved with as little work as possible.

The man who would soon move to the States and change his name to Charles was a small man in stature, but even in his early adulthood, his charm and charisma were legendary among the locals. He was becoming a man who could sell garlic to a vampire simply by using his words, but like Stanford almost a century after him, his tongue was so twisted it could have opened a wine bottle.

Also, similarly to Sir Allen, Ponzi left his university with little credentials, empty pockets, and a staunch belief that he was a burgeoning big shot. He needed to be seen as a high-roller, and he would do anything it took to rise to the top of the financial and, in turn, social ladder. We will see throughout this section on Charles Ponzi that the similarities with Stanford and all the other investment schemers are endless.

Other students at the University of Rome were, for the most part, very wealthy. Their families had paid their way easily, and unlike Ponzi, who had slipped in on the coattails of the last remnants of cachet attached to his surname, these young men had cash on the hip to enjoy the finer things between lectures. It would later be said that Ponzi insisted on tagging along with them when they frequented snazzy bars and upscale restaurants, blowing what little money he had trying to be seen as one of the upper-class. This insecurity would drive him to manipulate and steal his way to wealth.

Like many Europeans at the time, word had been filtering back for years of the fortunes to be made across the Atlantic. In America, a man could go out in the morning with 50 cents in his pocket and come back home that evening with five bucks if they had guile and determination. It was the Land of the Free, the Land of Opportunity, and the ideal place for someone like Ponzi to grift his way to fortune.

On the 3rd of November 1902, young Charles Ponzi landed on the docks of Boston with his life savings already squandered. Having gathered enough funds to set himself up on his arrival, Ponzi had spent the whole trip from Italy to the States gambling with the other passengers. After his arrest years later, he told a New York Times reporter that he "landed in this country with $2.50 in cash and $1 million in hopes, and these hopes never left me" (Darby, 1998).

If we're being kind, Ponzi was a dreamer, but when we look at it more realistically, he was simply a thief who wanted nothing

53

more than total wealth with none of the hard work. As we will see, Ponzi stole from people from any walk of life, and if there was an opportunity to take five bucks off a struggling family, he did so as casually as he would snatch a cheque for fifty grand from an aristocrat. He didn't discriminate, and there was no Robin Hood-type creamy centre to his dealings, only a rock-hard, selfish shell.

He was a fast learner and, by all accounts, an intelligent man. But he mostly relied on his charm to get by, and he had an endless supply of that. Ponzi learned English a few months after setting foot on American soil and worked several low-paying jobs along the East Coast, always waiting for one opportunity that would lift him above all of his fellow grafters.

It would be nearly two decades before that chance arrived, but Ponzi still found himself in some very entertaining scrapes along the way. One of his first jobs was as a dishwasher at a snobby Boston restaurant. While there, he spent most nights sleeping on the floor of the foyer as he had no home, but he soon managed to impress the management enough to land the slightly easier position of waiter.

His new role didn't last, and he was soon caught skimming the customers' change and straight-up stealing from the till. He was fired, and the trend of his life was truly in motion, and his view on life decided: If left in the care of other people's money—anyone at all—he would take it. He felt no remorse for this, even in his later years, and as with all thieves, genuinely believed he was entitled to whatever his heart desired.

After several years of having little to no luck on the East Coast, Ponzi packed his tiny clothes up and headed north to Canada, specifically Montreal. By now, he had added French to his knowledge of Italian and English, and through these skills and his unbelievable charm, he got a job at a bank—the Banco Zarossi (BZ).

The BZ had been set up in Canada to deal with the finances of the many Italian immigrants who had found their way to Montreal over time, and it is said that here, Ponzi actually worked quite hard, at least on the face of things. Regardless, he quickly climbed his way up to the position of the bank's manager, proving there was real grit and intelligence in the man if he'd only focused these qualities on the straight and narrow.

Unbeknownst to BZ's investors at the time, the bank was in danger of going under. Ponzi hadn't known this when he'd started, and the financial straits they found themselves in were nothing to do with him, it must be clarified. But what he did do was observe the tactics the owners used in their vain attempts to pay back their crippling debts: They offered unheard-of and impossible-to-sustain returns on new investors' cash deposits if they chose BZ as their bank. Of course, this angle will sound familiar to us—it is basically Stanford's certificate of deposit grift —and it rang a bell for Ponzi too.

What the bank's owners tried to do was use the new investors' money to pay off their more pressing debts, but of course, it only brought new debt that would have to be faced in the near future. It is the epitome of robbing Peter to pay Paul, and it is the very crux of a Ponzi scheme. It shows that this tactic had been around before the man himself used it, but as mentioned, it hadn't been done on such a grand scale yet.

Unfortunately for Ponzi—and the thousands of investors in his own scheme years later—he was back to square one. Jobless, penniless, and without scruples, Ponzi began calling to the doors of the wealthier clients he had dealt with during his short spell as manager of BZ in the hopes of securing work. On one occasion, he knocked on the door of the offices of a transportation company he'd corresponded with previously. Finding that the premises were empty for the day, he snuck inside, found the owner's cheque book, and wrote himself one for a fairly hefty amount.

Being the man he was, Ponzi then took to recklessly spending the money at will on drinks, fancy meals, and all the things that went with looking important. His blowout alerted the local authorities, who quickly arrested him, and he was sentenced to three years in prison for fraud. He served his time and was released in 1911, and then decided his time in Canada was up and moved back to the United States.

Not long after arriving, he fell into more illegal activity and began working for a firm that smuggled Italian immigrants into America through Canada. He was caught again and spent another couple of years in prison, and upon his release, tried to set up his own businesses. Some of these were legitimate attempts, but none of them had any structure, and they all came crashing down quite quickly.

Back in Boston, he rented a small office with little idea of what he would actually use it for. Again, we are seeing someone who needs to be seen as something he's not, but also aware enough to know that image goes a hell of a long way. He began sending letters to businesses in Europe in an attempt to make contacts he could use in any way to make a real go at earning his fortune. He had no real plan and nothing to offer, but he was an opportunist and just needed the right chance to come along.

One letter from a company in Spain changed everything, and Ponzi received something that would change his life forever.

What the company sold or did, we don't know, and whatever Ponzi had suggested as a business opportunity has been lost too.

But none of that mattered because it was what came in the envelope alongside the letter that set the wheels of what we now know as his Ponzi scheme in motion.

An International Reply Coupon (IRC) was how large companies from other countries would get people to correspond with them. If a company in Spain wanted a reply from a potential customer or client in another country, they couldn't expect them to pay for their own stamps to send a letter. Also, the company couldn't send stamps from their own land as they wouldn't work, so what they did was send these IRCs. These could be used to purchase stamps in any country, ensuring the recipient replied, or at least was more likely to.

Following World War I, many European nations were still in turmoil. For companies in places like Italy to purchase an IRC, they could pay 1 cent American, and once sent over to the States, these coupons could be cashed in for 5 cents worth of stamps. Of course, there was a clear loophole to make a profit, but someone would have to find a way to get thousands of IRCs sent over, cash them in for stamps, and then go to the effort of selling the stamps on the street.

Technically, the grift would work, but realistically, it wasn't feasible. Still, Ponzi smelled a scheme, and he set about spreading the word that he had found a glitch in the system that allowed for a staggering 50% return on any investment in the space of two months. He was clever, though, and he made sure to only "let this secret slip" over drinks at snazzy bars or during lunch with a wealthy acquaintance. He knew this would make it more appealing and also make it sound a lot more legitimate.

This is where the Ponzi scheme as we know it today was born. So far as we know, he only ever made $60 out of the IRC grift itself, but it was the perception of what it could do for people that caught the imagination. Ponzi simply used the idea of it to trick investors into giving him their money. The first ten of them gave him around $100 each, and he paid them their $150 two months later, as he had promised. But a Ponzi scheme is all about smoke and mirrors, and the majority—if not all—of these people instantly reinvested their money, so essentially, their profits were nothing more than Ponzi's words.

The idea of all Ponzi schemes is to convince people they are making money hand over fist, when in reality, each investor is only seeing someone else's money, and only from a distance at that. For the rare few who wanted to cash out, Ponzi paid them. As his intake exploded, he was taking in more money than he ever dreamed, so slicing a sliver off his stacks to reassure a client was actually an investment of sorts, as it advertised his business as being completely above board.

Several investors had come back to their wine clubs and cigar shops with dollar signs dancing like sugar plums before their eyes, telling everyone who would listen that the tiny Italian with the fancy offices in downtown Boston was a financial wizard. Ponzi changed his company name to the Security Exchange Company and registered it as a legitimate business, made house calls to Boston's wealthiest people, and hired agents to do the same. He took money from anyone and everyone, and all based on his promise of a 50% return on a seemingly endless supply of 5-cent IRCs. It was all a smokescreen, and on paper, there really could be an 80% profit made on the stamps. But to physically ship and sell them at any conceivably real profit was impossible, yet Ponzi's charm and secrecy about how he would actually manage it won investors over. Also, as we've seen, he paid out on one every so often just to show how honest the whole operation ran.

To put into perspective exactly how rapidly Ponzi's scheme grew, we have to look at it in terms of growth from inception to its bust, which was basically an eight-month period. He started the company in January of 1920 with 10 investors each giving him around $100. He paid these guys their money with the first trickling of new investors, and word spread. Between February and March, it went from a $5,000 investment to $25,000 (the equivalent of $75,000 to $350,000 in 2022, respectively). Ponzi hired even more agents to rope in people, spreading his net over the New England region and New Jersey.

Six months after starting, he had taken in $450,000 ($5,800,000 in 2022), and staggeringly, by June, it had risen to an eye-watering $2,500,000 ($34,000,000 in 2022). At the start of July, he was making a million dollars a week, and by the end of it, a million dollars a day.

Ponzi's initial investors were poor immigrants such as himself. Shamelessly, he convinced them to re-mortgage homes, hand over life savings, and sell family heirlooms, anything he could do to make them hand over money. He crippled generations of people, stole from the rich, gave to himself, and did it all without ever reinvesting a penny. Every cent was just money floating around while being passed from one victim to the next, with Ponzi pocketing the millions that people—approximately 90% of them—reinvested.

He bought mansions, ate at the best restaurants, and was known to be seen walking down the street with a gold cane in his munchkin hands. Ponzi was living the life he'd always demanded he should have, and he was doing so using thousands of other people's money. When it all came crashing down, he took with him several banks and many smaller businesses that had believed his spiel.

Charles Ponzi's scheme only lasted until August of the same year he started it, and when everything he had constructed collapsed, investors are said to have lost $20,000,000 ($199,000,000 in 2022). Amazingly, he only served three and a half years in prison and spent the rest of his life attempting cons in America, Italy, and Brazil.

A Ponzi scheme is essentially a huckster's card trick at a local fair, except on a much grander scale. It is all about what people think they see, and when it comes to money, most will see what the grifter tells them to see. For people like Carlo Pietro Giovanni Guglielmo Tebaldo Ponzi, Bernard Madoff, and Sir Allen Stanford, who they steal from or how devastating it will be to their future doesn't matter one iota. They want to be rich, and to them, other human beings are just a means to an end.

When these types of con artists take someone's cash, they only reinvest it in themselves and their lavish lifestyle while forever promising that the money is safe and gaining interest in their company. Whenever the investor or depositor (or whatever the grift entails) wants their money, they are convinced that reinvesting will be guaranteed to make it grow further. They are shown records of how much they are making and, in Allen Stanford's case, waltzed around a state-of-the-art building in Houston or Antigua.

They are essentially hoodwinked, and saying that a fool and their money are soon parted might be a little harsh, given how smooth and conniving these guys are.

Although several tried before him and many after, Charles Ponzi is for whom the scam is named, so most see him as the granddaddy of such schemes. Sir Allen Stanford worked his particular one over a much longer period of time and therefore reaped the benefits of it throughout most of his adult life. Still, without the likes of Ponzi paving the way, the big Texan might have just ended up working at his local Walmart, although that is pretty hard to imagine.

The Mind of Allen Stanford

As we come back to the main story of Allen Stanford, we need to understand just how his mind worked. We can never fully know what made him tick, but still, an insight into some of the decisions he made and the way he treated people will help us to at least grasp what was going through his head. Oftentimes, such outrageous behaviour is unfathomable to us regular folks, and it can become hard to rationalise it all as nothing but fantasy. To think there are people out there who spend $25 million on one party is simply outrageous, yet for Allen Stanford, it was just another weekend.

Around the time Stanford was celebrating the massively successful maiden Stanford 20/20, the government in Antigua and Barbuda needed a way to thank him. Unfortunately for him, they couldn't actually make him a god, so instead, they bestowed the title of 'Sir' on him. The Earl of Essex, Prince Edward, joined the Governor-General of Antigua and Barbuda, Sir James Carlisle, and made the announcement during the Silver Jubilee Independence Day Celebration. For those who worked with the Texan at the time, he is said to have been over the moon with his new name and revelled in being referred to as Sir Allen. This is one of our main insights into how he functioned as a human being.

For most of us, the idea of becoming a Knight of the Realm in Britain or a Sir on the Caribbean Islands is so far-fetched we have never once realistically considered it, but for the likes of Allen Stanford, such ridiculousness is always something they believe achievable, if not a God-given right. Also, the majority of people would not only refuse to consider such a thing, but it would probably mean very little to us if it were to happen. In fact, many would find it embarrassing.

Allen Stanford's need to be seen as the Big Cheese never left him, and as things grew to unimaginable proportions, so did the scale of grandeur needed to impress him and give any form of satisfaction. Fancy cars, big houses, airlines, and billions to spend were only the bare minimum of what was expected. If the Forbes Richest List had 38 people ahead of him, Stanford would feel 38 times smaller than the guy at the top. Life is a competition to narcissists, and the only way to win is to throw bigger parties, flash more cash, and be seen out and about with the most exclusive celebrities.

Nothing is beyond a man who genuinely called his dog RAS, as in, Robert Allen Stanford. These little tidbits are so outrageous they border on insanity, but with everything else we know about Stanford, naming his dog after his own initials is somehow one of the less shocking stories concerning him. When stacked up against the $20 million cricket game, his adultery, and dodgy business dealings, this sort of behaviour seems almost natural.

Laurie-Ann Holding, whose management company had organised the 20/20 for Stanford, spoke of his eccentricities, mood swings, and nasty temper. In one instance, Sir Allen demanded the global superstar and Jamaican musical god Sean Paul perform at one of his parties. When told how much it would cost, Stanford flicked a wrist at such suggestions and demanded the reggae rapper be there the following night to entertain his guests.

Now, we need to remember that in the early noughties, Sean Paul was at the top of his game, having scored several number one slots on the Billboard Top 100. Apart from his success around the world, in the Caribbean Islands, he was fervently loved, and most of all, he wasn't cheap. But for Stanford, the musician was just another commodity he could throw cash at to make him dance to his tune.

In an interview on the BBC's Sport's Strangest Crimes podcast, Laurie-Ann recalled how Stanford had scoffed at any suggestion that getting Sean Paul on such short notice would be impossible. When informed the rapper was playing a show in New York the night before and couldn't be there in time, Sir Allen simply creased his brow at her perceived ignorance and told her to send one of his planes.

Stanford's party went ahead the following night, with Sean Paul on centre stage.

Sparing one of his aeroplanes wouldn't have been much of a hindrance for Stanford. Remember, he had his own airline in Antigua, and by the time of his arrest and subsequent audit, he was found to own six private jets too. Yes, the man had actually acquired a fleet!

Along with his collection of aircraft, Stanford had homes in Houston, Antigua, and Florida, with the latter costing a cool $10 million. He also had another house in the same state he rented for his ex-wife, who stayed there thanks to Stanford paying a staggering $10,000 per week on rent. Sir Allen didn't mind spending exorbitant amounts of money because every penny of it was someone else's. Much like Charles Ponzi, absolutely no regret or shame ever entered his mind.

Stanford also owned a couple of yachts, with the most obnoxiously big one costing 100 grand a week. Purchases such as this are usually reserved for the top 1% on the planet, which Stanford was not. In fact, he was essentially broke since the only money he spent belonged to others, but such small details were never really an issue for him.

Allen Stanford's extravagant spending didn't end with fancy boats and houses, not even close. There was the $25 million party held back in the States for his board members, senior staff, and most importantly, potential investors. Sir Allen spared no expense, and according to all reports, the whole weekend would have made Lady Gaga blush.

One of Sir Allen's 24/7 camera operators later explained that Stanford booked out an entire hotel in downtown Manhattan for the weekend. The guests were treated to an expensive meal at a Michelin-starred restaurant before being taken to a nightclub which had been redecorated to look exactly like Studio 54, with everything from Andy Warhol lookalikes to naked women riding horses. But possibly the most 'Stanford' of all the ridiculousness on show was the Broadway musicians and groups who were hired to sing Stanford-themed songs, all the way down to lyrics about his investment group and banks.

We've mentioned Stanford's alimony, and in a previous chapter, we heard about his "outside wives" from none other than the man's own father. Still, apart from the money he had to shell out to keep them all in Armani, getting married so many times and siring at least six kids is more indicative of how Stanford functioned. He was dismissive of such things; to him, wives and children were just playthings, something he could parade around when needed and then lock away from the public eye when the deed was done.

The wonderful Laurie-Ann Holding tells another story of when Stanford's complete lack of empathy was fully on show. In the build-up to one of his 20/20 games, Sir Allen walked out onto the pitch to introduce his son to the crowd. The boy in question—or at least the one who thought he was—had been over for a visit and was sitting in the director's box. When Stanford announced to the onlookers that his son was about to join him on the pitch, the poor lad in the box stood up, only to see a sibling he'd never known existed sheepishly shuffling out and into the bear-hug embrace of his beaming pop.

An incident such as this would go down in any regular family's history as the main talking point over every Christmas dinner that followed. Yet, in Stanford's life, it was just another day at the office. He lived minute by minute, and if he felt like doing something, he did so with zero trepidation or forethought. To him, he paid these kids' alimony so that he could do whatever he pleased, whenever he pleased.

In an interview from his prison cell years later, Allen would get weepy when he spoke of the injustices of how he had been unfairly painted as a terrible father in the media. The term "crocodile tears" always springs to mind when picturing this scene, and as is often the case with criminals and straight-up bad people once their cover is blown, he played the 'misunderstood' card with impunity. Stanford was an expert at acting surprised when he stepped on people's toes, as was shown in his blatant attempts to justify what he was doing to the sport of cricket.

As we will discuss in more detail later, Stanford had steered clear of moving his grift over to America for a long time. Of course, we know this was because of the regulations and constant audits he'd have to face, but it could be said that he loved being a big fish in a small pond. In Antigua—and the whole of the Caribbean, really—Stanford was the wealthiest person there. He had billions more than the prime minister, Lester Bird, and therefore was essentially more powerful than him too. Why would he go to America and become just an average ol' billionaire when he could quite literally live like a god on the islands?

Like all narcissists, the Stanford seen on TV or in public was nothing like the man that existed behind closed doors. On camera, he was eccentric, charming, and even likeable in a weird way. He knew what to say and when to say it, and his enthusiasm could be infectious. At the time, there would have been several people watching who knew the real man, but they were usually wives, employees, and close friends. Although, even the majority of those who worked for him were oblivious to the sheer extent of how rotten his SFG company was at its core.

In private, the Sir Allen Stanford people got to know was aggressive and nasty. In one incident during the promotional tour of his maiden 20/20 tournament, Stanford had demanded that Laurie-Ann's management company gather all of the top players from the 19 nations participating in the competition for a huge press conference in front of the world's media. There, he would have several speakers stand up on stage and wax lyrical about the festivities to come and, of course, heap praise on the man who was organising it all.

The last person to speak was going to be Sir Allen, obviously, but by the time the giant Texan had sauntered onto the stage, the microphone had been lowered, unbeknownst to him. Sir Allen liked to stand up straight with his chest out when he addressed a crowd in order to get his booming voice out there, so the mic ended up even further from his mouth. It took 20 minutes for a shaking employee in the crowd to mention that they couldn't hear him, and Sir Allen was enraged.

The story goes that he charged into the offices directly after his speech, flipped a desk, and threw his glass of beer at someone's head, only missing them by inches. He roared, ranted, and threatened everyone in attendance and more than once referred to the amount of money he was spending. To Stanford, the only voice worth hearing at the event had quite literally gone over everyone's head, and that was sacrilege in itself.

Another narcissistic and sociopathic trait Stanford clearly possessed was a belief that if he said something was so, it became gospel. He was famed for destroying laptops if he got an email containing bad news and, on more than one occasion, hurled them into the sea when given particularly troubling information. Although we can't ever get inside his head fully, tossing a computer into the ocean in order to make a problem go away is bordering on lunacy. But like all self-centred psychos, Stanford probably believed if he didn't want the issue to be there, it would go away.

His approach to being audited was the same, although he gave it a little more thought than flinging a laptop into the Caribbean sea. Althea Crick, a banking regulator on Antigua at the time of Stanford's infamous years there, became known as one of the only members of the Regulatory Committee he could never manage to get in his pocket. Her persistence in thoroughly auditing his Stanford International Bank (previously Guardian International Bank) was a constant thorn in his side, and at one point, he had her transferred to another island for a month as her findings began to turn up information he needed to remain buried.

Stanford eventually had her fired in 2002. Now he could have all his 'audits' done by Leroy King, a man he had taken a blood oath with not long before Miss Crick began clamping down on his bank. King would rubber-stamp anything Stanford needed, and from then on, he could simply move his money around any way he wished. The whole fiasco gives us yet another insight into Stanford's way of thinking: If he was ever in danger of being exposed as a fraud, he bought the problem away.

To give Althea Crick her dues, she never once shied away from the situation and even stood up in court years later and testified against the billionaire thief.

"I'm not a yes person," she told the jury, referring to a time in 1998 when Stanford tried to pressure her into ignoring the irregularities in his bank's books. "And I don't rubber-stamp" (Driver, 2012).

Leroy King, for his part, would be charged as a co-conspirator in 2009, and Althea's loyalty and honour would finally be rewarded when she was named chairperson of Antigua's Financial Services Regulatory Commission. Her view on Stanford never wavered, and she once described the way he ran his business and his insatiable greed as "the rat being put in charge of the cheese" (Driver, 2012).

The world Allen Stanford had created for himself was nothing but a house of cards. He had stacked the deck well, sure, but in the end, everything he had built could never have lasted. Granted, he got two good decades of living it large before the walls caved in, and even then, he continued to vehemently deny any wrongdoing. In his mind, he deserved everything he had acquired, just not the justice he received for illegally obtaining it.

Thinking that his arrogance and narcissism blinded him from the crooked dealings going on behind the scenes of his SFG and Stanford International Bank (SIB) empires would be remiss. He knew everything that was being done to swindle money, and all of the significant decisions came directly through him. If he were as oblivious as he later claimed, he would never have made such moves as getting Althea Crick fired or stuffing the inner layer of a pile of bills before landing at Lord's.

Sir Allen was a grifter, a cheat, and a con artist. Any other description is being too kind. Of course, his outlandish claims and ostentatious spending can be seen in terms of entertainment, as some of his stories are so unbelievable they can be hard to take literally, but the aftereffects for the investors who went broke are very real. At the height of his Ponzi scheme, Stanford had defrauded over 300,000 people out of nearly $8 billion. Only $1 billion of that was ever accounted for, meaning he blew the rest on failed businesses, pet projects, and, of course, his cricket ventures.

Only a select few choose the path Allen Stanford went down, and when they make that decision, it is only ever going to bring them to one of two places: all or bust. We might laugh at how outrageous it all was, but when someone like Stanford lives a life in the manner he did, feathers will inevitably be ruffled at some stage.

Robert Allen Stanford learned this the hard way on the night the England team played their warm-up game against Middlesex in Antigua under the terrible floodlights, and as always, it was like nothing seen before.

The $20 Million Game

"Let me tell you this. Our cricket in the Caribbean is BACK!"

This was the boisterous claim of Sir Robert Allen Stanford as he stood in the centre of the pitch surrounded by the jubilant Stanford Superstars and a packed Stanford Cricket Ground crowd. That's a whole lot of 'Stanfords' for one sentence, but when the man himself put his name on everything he touched, it is impossible to avoid.

For the people watching back in England and around the globe, the sight of the billionaire Texan holding a microphone and sweating through his T-shirt as he proclaimed Caribbean cricket was 'BACK' would have been hard to take. The very sport he was referring to had just lost so much of its honour. In metaphorical terms, cricket at that moment in time was tucking a fistful of dog-eared bills in its garter belt and shuffling back to its lamppost.

The realisation that cricket had sold its soul to a talking moustache had manifested in the public's mind long before those now-infamous scenes. A few days before, as the England team played their warm-up match against Middlesex, Stanford had managed to outrage the players, fans, and media alike when he decided a good marketing ploy—or a power play, more likely—would be to get the camera operator to film him as he bounced the players' wives and girlfriends on his knee. It was a shocking sight, and to anyone watching at the time, everything to do with the Stanford Twenty/20 for Twenty had been damaged beyond repair.

The images of a smirking Stanford fondling the partners of Matt Prior, Alastair Cook, and Luke Wright were, at best, cringeworthy and, at worst, despicable cases of sexual harassment. Even those not involved in cricket were stunned, and the following morning's newspapers printed the story on the front pages rather than the back. Stanford's horrendous behaviour had surpassed the indignity of playing a match for a substantial amount of money, and in terms of publicity, it even put the sport of cricket on the backburner.

It was a moment in time that seemed to encapsulate exactly what YouTube was created for, and it summed up the man perfectly. As the players tried to concentrate on what was happening on the pitch, the big screen switched to an image of the grinning Texan and the three ladies. At that moment, James Anderson was about to bowl, and Matt Prior was keeping wicket. The sight of them looking up to see what was happening will be burned into the retinas of anyone who has seen the footage, and we can only imagine how the players themselves felt. The fact that Emily Prior was pregnant as Stanford bounced her on his knee only added to the shocking nature of what was happening.

Jonathan Agnew, the BBC's cricket correspondent, was covering the game at the time, and he summed it all up a year later when he explained the feeling in the stadium as the images changed on the big screen.

"It was obviously dark, and the floodlights were on and there's this big screen. I think it was Jimmy Anderson about to bowl, and he sort of turned at the end of his run and looked up at the screen," he told the Sport's Strangest Crimes podcast. "And Matt Prior, who was keeping wicket, looked up at the screen, and there's his wife with Allen Stanford all over her, and everything just stopped. And that was the moment I think they realised they'd sold their souls" (James, 2022).

The incident was world news, and Stanford had to act quickly to extinguish the fire. A dinner he had planned for the players after the Middlesex game was boycotted by the English boys, and news started to leak out about how enraged they were. Of course, the ECB tried everything they could to pin a smiley face badge over the cracks, but by then, it was already too late. When they spoke on behalf of the players and told the media it was just a misunderstanding and all was forgiven, they only poured salt into an already gaping wound.

Stanford held a press conference, where he attempted to explain away his behaviour as an innocent misunderstanding. In typical narcissistic style, he blamed the camera operator, who he claimed had orchestrated the whole debacle. He told reporters he was going to "kick the guy's butt" and that he didn't even know the women had been the players' wives. Of course, even if this were true (it's not), it basically meant that if the ladies had been anyone but the players' partners, he would have had total freedom to treat them as he wished.

Even if the England players had wanted to pull out of the whole thing then, they couldn't have done. The contracts had been signed, and the players were already sailing down the River Styx without a paddle. Some in the England camp had already started to believe they were going to lose the game against the Superstars anyhow, so the added pressure of feeling like they had sold out must have been overwhelming, especially since they would probably receive no actual money for the dirty deed when they didn't win.

The Stanford Superstars looked sharp and ready, whereas England had barely scraped by against a supposedly much weaker Middlesex side. They could blame the lights—which genuinely were extremely poor—but there were far more issues inside the camp than simply that. Still, ex-players and pundits had latched onto the whole floodlight element very early on in the tour and continued to swat away questions about their poor performance with the measly excuse.

After the Middlesex game, Nasser Hussain, Michael Atherton, and the Sky Sports crew filmed a segment out on the pitch in order to justify the floodlight element. During the match, several players had dropped balls that seemed easier to catch, and the sports presenters wanted to test out the conditions. On live TV, they attempted to do what the players had failed in doing and confirmed afterwards that the floodlights made it almost impossible to see the ball until it was inches from their faces.

As it turned out, Stanford had found that the lower lights made for better aesthetics, as the silver stumps and bright kits glowed on the screen. It was just more proof he was only interested in appearances, and yet another dagger had been stuck into the heart of cricket as a result of his needs. It was a dagger being wielded by a billionaire, sure, but the ECB had made a decision that in no way benefited cricket as an institution, so they hadn't a leg to stand on.

For the West Indian islands, the money Stanford had been flashing around in the past had been put to good use, it must be said. As we have already covered, the Windies had been afforded new grounds, financial backing at a grassroots level, and over a quarter of a million dollars to each island for their cricket growth. The players would have seen the Twenty/20 for Twenty games as the time for some of the money to go to them, and that is completely fair.

Cardigan Connor would later reflect on the preparations of the West Indies players in the six weeks leading up to the game and spoke in glowing terms of the money spent. The islanders, who were used to basic training, were given everything they needed to get into perfect shape, and the results showed on the pitch. Of course, it could be viewed that the eventual prize money on the Stanford game would mean more to the West Indians, given that they earned less throughout their careers in general. Still, when we look back on the match itself when it finally rolled around, the Stanford Superstars were far superior throughout, regardless of the added incentive.

Along with the nasty media coverage circulating back in Britain even before a ball was bowled, the players on both sides had to put up with the pressure of playing for such a life-changing amount of money. They weren't just trying to win the cash for themselves, but for their teammates too, so who would want to be the man to make the mistake that lost it all for his fellow players? Luke Wright explained how much fear the players had going into the game.

"Oh yeah, I've never felt anything like it," he told the BBC's Sport's Strangest Crimes podcast. "I was physically sick on the morning of the game, even though I didn't have huge confidence in us winning anyway. Still, it was more like, don't lose it, and don't be the person that ends up costing your team that amount of money."

But the Stanford Super Series was always going to happen, so the players had to try and make the most of the ECB's greedy decision, regardless of how they felt. When the time came for the game to start, TV coverage was huge, and with the world watching, Stanford's vision came to life in a horrific fashion.

In front of the watching world, the Windies players demolished their English opponents from start to finish. With brightly coloured kits for the visitors and sharp black and green ones for the Superstars, the game again took place under the poorly lit lights that became synonymous with proceedings. Things looked good for England when they won the coin toss, but unfortunately for them, that was the only success they had. Everything after that went downhill fast.

Choosing to bat first (using the all-black Stanford-designed bats), they barely made a dismal 99 all out from 19 ½ overs. It was a hammering of the highest standard and humiliation the English wouldn't soon forget. After the knee-bouncing antics a few days prior (distasteful pun, I know), and the indignity of having taken part in the series at all, it looked like the players were going to be left to carry the ECB's mess on their shoulders and with not an extra penny to lighten the load.

By the time the Superstars were batting, they had finished the job less than an hour after stepping out into the middle. Andre Fletcher and captain Chris Gayle beat the life out of England, with the latter slamming a Freddy Flintoff bowl into the crowd to win with a devastating six. In the end, Stanford's Frankenstein creation ran out easy winners with a massive 10-wicket victory.

Stanford made a beeline for the pitch—and the cameras, of course —and amidst the jubilant celebrations of 11 brand new millionaires, he told the world that Caribbean cricket was back! For real cricket fans, they would have known the Windies had dominated the sport long before he showed up, and regardless of the slump they had been in during the late 90s, one match at the Stanford Cricket Ground wasn't the turning point he proclaimed.

Although the match was short-lived, the story surrounding it and, of course, that of Stanford himself was really the most interesting part.

From the poor floodlights to the stack of cash in a Perspex box, it was all a shambles from the word 'YEEHAW!'. The Windies boys would have seen it differently, but they had been looked after in ways the English never had. Their training, nutritionists, hotels, and everything else that came with being in Sir Allen's pocket far surpassed anything they'd ever experienced.

But what happened with the winnings? And how on Earth had the teams decided what way to split it?

These were some of the questions the cricket world, and especially the ECB, never considered. For the English, how to split the money should they win had been the cause of a lot of conflicts. Some players felt that the 11 men picked to play should be the sole receivers, while others thought the other four who were left out should get some of the cut. When the ECB signed their dignity over to Stanford, they clearly hadn't thought of the pressure that would be put on the selectors and the likes of captain Kevin Pietersen.

All the way up until the eve of the game, these decisions had yet to be made by the England camp, and on top of all of this, there was a genuine worry as to how the players should behave on the pitch if they won. With the recession tearing Britain and the rest of the world apart, the ECB was rightly worried about how it would look on TV if their players were jumping around and flashing cheques for a million dollars.

These fears were so pressing that they held a four-hour meeting to discuss just that: How should our players behave in the event of winning? Even before the actual Stanford Superstars v England XI game, the higher-ups knew they had made a mistake, but by then, they were in too deep. The press back home was already feeding the ECB and players' hearts to their hellhounds because of their lack of integrity, and images of Stanford playing Now What Do You Want for Christmas with the wives and girlfriends were everywhere.

As for the West Indies, the team that eventually won the money, it was even more life-changing than it might have been for the English lads. For their part, they had already decided on a split long before the game, with each of the 11 starting receiving $1 million apiece, the 4 men who missed out getting around $275,000 each, and the rest of the winnings being split between trainers, kit men, and staff.

Several of the Windies players had also decided to use the money to set their families up, with some of them sending sisters to America for college, paying for their hard-working parents to finally retire, or simply buying houses for loved ones. Unfortunately, many of them were convinced to reinvest the money in Stanford's certificates of deposit and, in the end, lost everything they had played for when Sir Allen went bust the following year.

As the English players hung their heads in the dressing room while the Superstars celebrated on the pitch, England Head Coach Peter Moores had the job of trying to raise spirits. Luke Wright, who was a young player at the time but fast on his way to being one of the main men, claimed the general point of Moores' team talk was about how the real privilege was playing for England and that no player grew up dreaming of representing their country in a Stanford Superstars match.

It probably did little to help the distraught players at the time, but then again, that old chestnut 'hindsight' needs to be mentioned again. When they look back on what Moores had to say now, it surely makes a little more sense. They had grown up dreaming of playing for England in test—and even the original Twenty20—cricket, and the Superstars game was just a sideshow. Whether he mentioned that the ECB had basically forced Stanford's plan on them all will forever stay in the dressing room, and rightly so, but we have to hope it was at least brought to their attention.

Not everyone was against the Stanford Super Series, though. Sports journalist Andy Bull was very vocal in his support of the event in his column in the Observer.

"English cricket was slow to accept that a player did not demean himself by making a living from sport. The great medium-pace bowler SF Barnes was left out by England between 1902 and 1907 because he preferred to earn money playing as a professional in the Lancashire League. Now it seems we are just unhappy that a player's skills can earn him a quick million" (Bull, 2008).

He went on to point out that even in 1697, before the ECB and cricket as we know it today even existed, matches were being played in Sussex for 50 guineas a man. That is the equivalent of £70,000 today, while Fredrick the Prince of Wales captained a side to defeat in 1735 for a pot of £1,000, a serious amount of readies in 2022. Money had been used as an incentive for centuries, Bull was determined to point out, so what difference if the man offering it was an annoying Texan.

Obviously, Mr. Bull became very sheepish on the subject a few months later when Stanford's empire collapsed like a red-top newspaper in a wind tunnel, but such behaviour is endemic in journalists. Even so, his point had some kernels of truth in it, at least in terms of what came before in the sport. Still, he was also referring to times when cricket wasn't a professional sport, so the majority of people who played it back then earned no money unless they played these paid games on the side. The players involved in the Twenty/20 for Twenty games were already earning a more than decent living.

The Stanford Superstars v England XI was only ever going to be farcical. From the moment the helicopter rotors cut through the blue sky over Lord's, through Stanford's knee-bouncing of the players' partners, all the way up until he celebrated with the players on the pitch, it never sat right. For one thing, it was organised by a con artist, and even with most of his shady dealings still just a file on an FBI agent's desk, enough was known about him for the ECB to steer clear.

Also, it must be taken into account that organisers on the British side of things seemed more concerned with how the players should act if they won, which only points to major trepidation and even guilt on their part. They knew what the risks were, yet they refused to look under the colossal moustache and acknowledge the sneer hidden just beneath it.

When cricket fans today look back on that night in Antigua, the majority do so with shrugged shoulders and an embarrassed smile. Even though they had no control over what happened, fans of sport—any sport—are almost like a hivemind. They live and breathe the good and the bad times as one, and when a stain such as Stanford's ruins the sheets, it soaks through into the skin of all involved.

Ironically, it is the higher-ups who made the bed that usually distance themselves from such scandals the quickest, and the ECB clearly decided to take this particular route. Instead of taking their lumps, they went about suing the Player's Association, who had come out and told the world they had forewarned the big wigs, namely David Collier, about the dangers of getting into bed with a man of Stanford's character. Such a knee-jerk reaction as taking the Association to court only condemned the ECB in everyone's eyes, but they needed to protect their own.

Whatever the reasons for Stanford's offer being accepted originally, the consequences had to be dealt with back home in the aftermath. When news broke a few months later that Guardian International Bank and Stanford were to be investigated by the FBI and Scotland Yard, hundreds of thousands of investors rushed to cash out, and in a weird way, the media scrutiny in Britain shifted from the ECB to the crux of the story: an S8 billion Ponzi scheme.

For Sir Allen Stanford, an orange jumpsuit awaited, and the real pantomime could begin.

The House of Cards Collapses

As the England players licked their wounds on the flight home from Antigua, the Stanford Superstars partied through the night. They had just won a life-changing amount of money for what was essentially one night's work, and the man who had declared he would bring Caribbean cricket back had apparently followed through on his outlandish promise.

Behind the scenes, things had been steadily falling apart inside the Stanford Financial Group (SFG) and everything connected to his Stanford International Bank (SIB). Even before the obnoxious cricket match between the Stanford Superstars and England XI, the man himself had been very aware of what he would undoubtedly call 'detractors' among his staff. In reality, they were just a few of the people working for SFG who actually had a conscience.

In June of 2008, the same month Sir Allen Stanford was landing a chopper on the Nursery Ground at Lord's, two former employees were taking separate routes to the Security and Exchange Commission (SEC) offices in Fort Worth with stacks of documents that could potentially bring their old moustachioed boss down for good. Mark Tidwell and Charlie Rawl had decided to stand up for their ethics and take on a billionaire, which in reality, is a terrifying prospect.

Both Rawl and Tidwell had been financial advisors to Stanford's SFG for several years, having been headhunted by the man himself. Of course, Stanford's most common reason for bringing

82

in new employees—especially in higher positions—was simply to get a piece of their already stocked client list. If he could get them over to SFG and SIB, then it meant connections and essentially more money for him, and that was all he cared about, really.

The two soon-to-be whistle-blowers had tolerated SIG's dodgy dealings for a period after their initial employment, but they had no idea how deep the illegal activity ran. Once they started to ask questions, things became uncomfortable, and the reality of Stanford's fraudulent scheme surfaced. By 2007 they had seen enough, but getting out from the tightening clutches of an iron-fisted billionaire isn't as simple as handing in your resignation, and Rawl and Tidwell soon found that if they were to take the high road, Sir Allen was going to put as many roadblocks as he could in front of them.

Although, one piece of luck would be on Rawl and Tidwell's side that day in 2007, as the SEC—whose job it is to investigate fraud and financial manipulation—had already been aware of Stanford's dealings through his Antiguan offshore bank. Of course, they had little on him by then, but at least the two men weren't walking into the offices in Fort Worth and starting from scratch.

The thread had started to be pulled on the fabric of Stanford's empire long before Rawl and Tidwell were left with no other option than to try to bring him down. A few years before, Sir Allen had decided to do the one thing he'd always sworn he wouldn't and moved in on American investors. Given the much stricter regulations and mandatory audits, not venturing into that market had been a smart move. Still, greed will make a person do irrational things, and it was this very trait Stanford possessed in spades which would be the beginning of the end for him.

We discussed before how a Ponzi scheme needs a constant influx of new investors to cover the old, and Stanford's was no different. By the time he'd started making plans to tap into the American public's pockets, older investors from his offshore accounts wanted their money. Not all of them, and no obvious red flags had been raised by then, but people who invest money, in general, will need it to come back out at some stage, whether they're buying a house, retiring, or simply moving their money somewhere else.

By the early 2000s, Stanford's offices in Houston were situated in one of the most modern—and it must be said, ostentatious—buildings in America. From the marble floors up to the Sistine Chapel-esque ceilings, it was glitz and glamour on a scale only Stanford could imagine. The building had spiral staircases with mahogany handrails and even a wall adorned with endless pictures of the giant Texan shaking hands with celebrities, American presidents, and world leaders. To any regular Joe or Jane walking in off the street, it would have been very easy to be conned into thinking the whole operation was kosher.

Stanford's need to show off was clear to anyone who stepped through the doors, but in a country where bigger always means better, it was the perfect spider web for trapping burgeoning retirees, who quickly became his primary targets. Stanford had decided early on that anyone's money would do—rich or poor—and retirees are often willing to roll the dice on what they have if there is a chance of making their golden years slightly more comfortable. Although, many of the lesser-off investors would have been trying to earn enough cash to see their children were looked after, which makes their losses all the more painful to accept.

Again, Stanford sold his CDs, only this time, he needed to show the people who were investing a lot more than he did for the drug cartels and money launderers. Back in the early years in Antigua, the people who 'invested' in his CDs needed to stay in the shadows, so a quick trip to the island to check out the premises was a big no-no. In America, Sir Allen was dealing with real, legal money, and the retirees looking to make 5% on their life savings wanted to be mesmerised before he felt them up in the cab on the way home.

Stanford knew this, and he wasn't just going to throw a plate of liver and onions in front of them and rub liniment oil into their bones while they watched Wheel of Fortune. Instead, he had his highest-rolling employees actually bus in hordes of older ladies and gentlemen and treated them to several hours of slides, videos, and entertainment at his swanky buildings in Houston and Miami. Essentially, he wowed them, and once they had signed up, the statements they received in the post were printed on the most expensive stationery, with fabricated numbers proclaiming their slow but steady profits. Once again, he used the word-of-mouth tactic, and he knew if one of the Golden Girls went back to their retirement village and told another about the 'guaranteed' growth of their investment, the temptation for others to sign up would be too hard to ignore.

One issue Stanford had to deal with was clearance from the banking regulators in the States, as bringing so many investors into such deals as CDs is a risky business, at least to those who understand how they work. So if a group like Stanford's SFG wanted to lure in investors for his proposal, the people signing up legally needed to have at least $1 million in provable assets. Like Charles Ponzi, Stanford wanted everyone's money, not just the wealthy, so he hired several high-priced lawyers to fight his corner.

The battle he was partaking in couldn't be won because he was 100% guilty of fraud, manipulation, and basically, simple theft. But Stanford didn't live that way, and as long as he kept the wolves from his door, he genuinely seemed to believe everything was hunky-dory. Even as the SEC began to sniff around his building in Houston, Stanford was still bringing in retirees by the coachload and flogging them his crooked CDs!

With CDs or any kind of investment, the money is meant to be reinvested in other supposedly guaranteed profitable ventures, but Stanford ran things differently. Sure, he invested in some ridiculous hotel ideas that fell flat on their faces, and he threw a ton of money at cricket events and his Antiguan airlines, but mostly what he invested other people's money in was himself. His houses, yachts, and ex-wives didn't come cheap, and what legitimate business choices he did make were disastrous.

By the mid-noughties, the SEC had taken to emailing thousands of Stanford's investors in order to try and start building some form of a paper trail. As mentioned already, taking on someone with the money and power at Sir Allen's disposal is a terrifying prospect because if you don't get him with the first shot, he is most definitely going to obliterate your life thereafter. Much like Roger 'Verbal' Kint says in The Usual Suspects, "How do you shoot the devil in the back? What if you miss?"

Once Rawl and Tidwell had decided to go up against Stanford and his investment group, they were truly on their own. When Charlie Rawl brought his concerns to one of Stanford's most trusted partners, he was told he was worrying over nothing. Rawl asked to see some of the paperwork concerning the clients he had brought over to SFG and was informed in no uncertain terms to keep his focus elsewhere.

After a private meeting with the man who would become his business partner years later, Rawl sat down with Mark Tidwell to discuss what they both were starting to see as a massive network of fraud. Of course, they had no idea how deeply it ran yet, or the astounding amount of money Stanford had bled out of the company to fund his own lavish lifestyle, but they knew things were gone past the point of rescuing.

Understanding that they might already be in too deep, Rawl made one last attempt to free himself when he walked into Stanford's office and told him he was leaving the company. Knowing Sir Allen's temper and vindictiveness, he decided to keep his concerns about the illegal activity at SFG and GIB to himself and simply informed Stanford he was quitting to concentrate on starting his own business.

Stanford dismissed him, and when Rawl went back and told a senior partner he was definitely done with the company, he was ordered to put his reasons for leaving down on paper. Again, Rawl just wanted a clean break, so he only wrote 10% of the shady things he had seen and feared would bring the company to its knees. When he showed up for work the following day to see out his last two weeks at SIG, he found his office had been locked and was informed that he had been fired.

From that moment, Rawl and Tidwell knew they were in a war.

Charlie Rawl told the Sport's Strangest Crimes podcast that he feared for his life by then, and even though Stanford never made a direct threat to him or his family's physical well-being, the potential for danger was always lingering.

"It literally became a David versus Goliath battle and the next fourteen to fifteen months were a living hell," he said, reminiscing about his harrowing ordeal of going up against Stanford. "They filed a lawsuit against us, and they fought to keep our clients, my client list, and my book of business I had built up over decades" (James, 2022).

Stanford only wanted the clients and the money they had to offer

—not the income they could bring to SFG or his apparent investments, but to fatten his own pockets and keep the clients from the previous investment rush happy. The whole operation was a Ponzi scheme from top to bottom, and the man running it was constantly digging downward while trying to climb out of the hole he found himself in.

"Stanford wanted to take my client list apart and distribute them out to his more loyal advisors. There is no doubt that he wanted to make an example out of the ones who had chosen to leave his company," Rawl told the podcast. He then went on to explain one of the intimidation tactics Stanford used. "I received a FedEx letter just prior to a Christmas party at my house. The letter said that I was fired and that I did not resign. That I was a liar and that Stanford would pursue every possible legal action against me. It was signed 'Merry Christmas'" (James, 2022).

Around the time Rawl and Tidwell were taking separate routes to the SEC offices in Fort Worth to report Stanford's Ponzi scheme, other employees were reportedly getting itchy feet too. As rumours of his house of cards being due a steady gust of wind from the authorities began to circulate, Stanford did what all smart businessmen would do in the same sticky situation; he reeled in the company's spending and laid low. Well, not exactly. This is Sir Allen Stanford, after all!

Instead of keeping his head down and trying to stem the flow of bad publicity that was starting to sprout around SIG, Stanford started throwing even larger parties and more regularly at that. He held obnoxious meetings where he called his most cut-throat performers up one by one and made a big deal of announcing the staggering bonuses they got that month. Numbers in the high five figures were not uncommon, and to anyone doubting how much money SFG and SIB were raking in, they only had to look to the end of the long table and see the cheques being handed out to the gushing sharks in suits and ties.

It was a classically sociopathic defence to take, and Stanford would have truly believed that if he insisted loud enough that everything was status quo, then it just had to be that way. He was hiding in plain sight, and anyone that doubted him was actually the crazy one. But even his lavish parties and ostentatious meetings couldn't hide the fact that his certificates of deposit were selling more than ever, and that meant there were more and more people who could claim their money back at any moment. When they found out Stanford had spent it on a single cricket game and yacht renovations, they must have been infuriated and terrified.

As 2008 became 2009, Stanford made one more colossal mistake. Not content with destroying the retirement and lives of Americans, he decided to move his grift overseas again. This time, he chose Libya, and he quickly set about hocking his CDs to the Libyan government and anyone else who would listen.

In January of 2009, he flew over to Tripoli with his most recent side-piece, Andrea Stoelker, to hammer out a deal with Muhammad Layas, the Chief Executive Officer of the Libyan Investment Authority. In a deal worth an estimated $500 million, Stanford returned home with more than enough money to keep his Ponzi scheme going for the foreseeable future. But he wasn't dealing with retirees this time, and within weeks, it is reported that the Libyans demanded their money back.

Even someone as arrogant as Allen Stanford would have known it was a bad idea to refuse their demands—some of the money belonging to the Gaddafis—Stanford returned the investments. With his latest round of cover investments gone, he had nothing to show for himself. The thread that had already been pulled to reveal nothing but a huckster's carnival trick beneath the shawl was fully torn away, and Stanford was left to face the music with his oversized Gucci pants around his ankles.

Along with the FBI's investigation, the SEC inquiries and even Scotland Yard's joint task force getting involved, the added pressure of the Libyan investment disaster was too much for even Sir Allen to cover up. Not long after, two of Stanford's most trusted employees were arrested, and as they started to appear on the rolling news channels in cuffs, Stanford panicked.

Once more, he went on the loudmouth offensive and told any daytime TV host or news reporter that he was innocent. He claimed that if he were really guilty, he would have been arrested already, and he predictably began to put the blame on those who had already been taken into custody, including his one-time best friend, Alan Davis.

True to form, he sang like a canary, chirping to all in sight that he was the poor, innocent victim who had only ever wanted to make people's savings grow. Stanford always stuck to his guns on this aspect, incessantly denying any knowledge of what had been happening at SIG, and he continued to do so in the years between his eventual arrest and trial... or at least until he claimed amnesia following an altercation with an inmate at Coleman II prison in Florida.

Almost fittingly, as the FBI closed in on his Houston building and the news channels began showing images of the company's computers and files being carried out by agents in navy flak jackets, the England cricket team were in Antigua to play a match against the West Indies. Unlike the embarrassing sideshow a few months before, this game held none of the glitz and glamour but all of the things that make cricket great.

For Stanford, his days of watching the sport and shouting into microphones on the pitch were coming to an end, and as the cuffs were getting nice and oiled in preparation for being slapped on his wrists, the house lights at the Stanford Show were flashing for the last call. It seemed his life in the fast lane was coming to an end, but Sir Allen—soon-to-be just plain ol' 'Allen' again—still had some extremely entertaining tricks up his sleeve.

The FBI and SEC Close In

So, the cricket game was done, and the players had flown home to try and forget everything that had happened in Antigua. Allen Stanford had travelled to Libya to wrangle more money to appease investors back in the States who were getting itchy feet, and the SEC was building a case that was getting more intriguing and shocking all the time.

In late April/early May of 2008, only a few months after the last ever ball was struck in a Stanford Twenty/20 for Twenty match, the SEC contacted the FBI in Texas and asked them to come in on the Stanford investigation. By now, the SEC had put a watch on Alan Davis—Stanford's right-hand man and confidant—and they were also becoming suspicious of Laura Pendergest-Holt, a young woman in her mid-thirties who had risen from a local member in Alan Davis's Bible study group to Chief Financial Officer (CFO) in Stanford's banking and investment operations seemingly overnight.

In true Days of Our Lives style, Davis had begun an affair with Pendergest-Holt a couple of years before and continued it throughout her tenure with GIB. Her being half his age was probably the sole attraction, given how much Davis continually tried to emulate Stanford in everything he did. Still, it was his hiring her to fill a position she was not in any way qualified for that would prove devastating in the trial that followed.

Meanwhile, the FBI had started to take a much closer look at Stanford and his businesses, and they heard alarm bells ringing very early on. What tickled their antennas first off was Stanford's board of directors, as not one of them possessed any form of banking or financial credentials. The Feds knew this only pointed to one thing: They were simply faces who were there to rubber-stamp any crooked papers Stanford needed to be approved.

After a little more digging, the FBI and SEC discovered that one of the members of Stanford's board was a man who had suffered a massive heart attack seven years before their investigation and had been in a coma ever since. Still, this poor guy was registered as an active member of the board and had somehow managed to sign important documents and clearance notices for SIG's CDs in the seven years that he had been unresponsive.

Another red flag for investigators was when they found out that Stanford's promised returns on clients' investments never wavered. Not once in over two decades did he change his original offer. The chances of such a percentage remaining fixed forever despite fluctuating markets, financial crashes, and everything else that goes with handling massive amounts of money was just an impossibility.

One roadblock for the investigators was the worrying discovery that nobody had ever really complained about Stanford's companies. In fact, everyone who banked or invested with him spoke well of their experiences. Of course, this was simply because the letters and statements they received each week informed them that their money was growing steadily and all was well. If they'd known the truth—that Stanford was just barely keeping things together from one round of investments to the next—they would have viewed it a whole lot differently.

Their first soberingly bitter taste of realisation came when ex-employee Charlie Rawl did an interview with Bloomberg News in May of 2008. The man who had gone to the SEC with his good friend Mark Tidwell late the previous year had been assured the interview he was about to give was off the record. Instead, in classic journalistic sleaziness, they lied through their teeth and within minutes of Rawl's words being spoken, they had been splattered across the internet for everyone—including the moustachioed Texan—to read.

Rawl told Bloomberg that he and several other employees had been left with no other ethical choice but to get out of Stanford's company. They feared for their clients and their futures, and Rawl explained that the way things were being run at SIB was far from above board. The interview sent shockwaves through the network of investors who had pumped money into Stanford's CDs and banks, and massive queues soon formed outside his offices in Houston, Miami, and Antigua.

A few months before his interview, Charlie Rawl had been dragged into the FBI offices and interrogated. He claimed there had been two agents, three SEC guys, and three criminal prosecutors in the room with him. At first, they pressed him aggressively, asking questions and making Rawl feel like he was the one who had done something wrong. Later, he admitted he quickly understood that all they were doing was making sure he was a credible witness. Still, a seven-hour interrogation by the FBI must have been a harrowing experience.

By now, the Feds knew something was rotten inside the Stanford empire, and they approached their higher-ups in order to ask for a permit to set up a sting operation. They needed Allen Stanford himself to be seen on tape selling his CDs to someone, but unfortunately, he only personally dealt with the extremely wealthy investors. His company still took money from anyone with two pennies to rub together, but that aspect of the fraud was left to his minions to carry out.

In order for the FBI to get a suitable undercover prospect, they needed someone who actually possessed a certain amount of money in their bank accounts. For people like Stanford, knowing precisely who is on the world's richest lists is an essential part of their existence, and Sir Allen would have known if the person coming to him to discuss an investment was genuinely wealthy or not. The Feds never could find a suitable candidate, and the sting operation idea was abandoned before it ever really took off.

Instead, they refocused their attention on Alan Davis and Laura Pendergest-Holt. The former had aged dramatically by then, and from all accounts of the SEC agents who monitored him in the final weeks before his arrest, he seemed defeated and ready to talk. But the investigators wanted Stanford in the clutches, and even though Davis had committed massive fraud too, using him to fry the bigger fish was seen as the more bankable approach. They knew they only had one shot, and an arrest that backfired would surely see Stanford slip out of their grasp for good. He was a master at disappearing when he needed to, and even with his assets frozen, he could easily have had hundreds of millions stashed away in an offshore account unbeknownst to the FBI.

Stanford's lawyers acted quickly and knew that without complaints from clients and investors on the record, the FBI and SEC probably had nothing to arrest their client on. Still, they could also see that the walls were closing in, and as a sign of good faith, Stanford offered up their Chief Financial Officer to answer any questions the authorities might have. Again, this was a staggeringly arrogant decision from an egomaniac who didn't even acknowledge that his CFO knew absolutely nothing about finance and, more damningly, even less about the workings of Stanford's banks.

The interrogators were shocked as the most basic questions directed at Laura Pendergest-Holt were answered with a blank stare or a shrug of the shoulders. It quickly became apparent she was clueless about the workings of GIB and SIG, but her need to close her eyes and block her ears throughout the shady dealings didn't make her innocent. The CFO might not have known the finer details of how the investors were being fleeced, but she sure as hell knew it had been happening and had become quite wealthy from it too.

In a move that seemed quite basic yet became surprisingly effective in the case, the FBI decided to give Laura what they call a "perp walk". This is when the agents take the perpetrator out of the Paddy Wagon in front of the watching—and presumably tipped off—media and march them from the vehicle to the station. The orange jumpsuit and cuffs only added to the whole scene, and for anyone looking at it unfolding through their television sets, it seemed clear that the bad guys would soon be doing the same thing. It all would have been especially damning for those involved in Stanford's shady dealings.

Alan Davis wasn't just witnessing one of his peers being led into the police station; he was watching his side-piece being arrested. It all became too much for him, and with his health hanging by a thread—and his marriage in the same condition, we have to assume—Stanford's old college pal and bona fide Mini-Me walked into a Texas police department headquarters and handed himself in to the authorities.

Now the Feds had two of the most prominent players in Stanford's game in custody, and unlike Laura Pendergest-Holt, Davis fully knew about every crooked deal, backhanded bribe, and cold-hearted swindle that had ever been done in his 20 years working with Sir Allen. The Federal agents and SEC guys listened with their jaws on the floor as Davis casually owned up to everything they'd done, and as each new piece of evidence gathered in a pile, everyone knew it was nearly time to bring the Big Dog in.

Allen Stanford knew his time was running out, and in a move that was so him it seemed made up, he flew all of his outside wives and children out to Napa County, California, for a holiday in a lodge he owned. Most of the women and children were meeting each other for the first time, and it is truly mind-boggling to try and grasp just how someone could envision such an event going well. But for Sir Allen, no such quandaries existed in life, and if he said everyone should have a sing-song and a jolly ol' time, well then that was precisely what they would do for him, regardless of how they felt.

All of this was happening while the SEC had announced they were charging Robert Allen Stanford with "massive ongoing fraud". It seems fitting that the charges came with such an obnoxious title, but the image of Stanford sipping wine surrounded by at least five of his wives and mistresses while his empire collapsed is hard to wipe away. It is utter egomania, and we can only wonder if he had finally managed to accept that things were going wrong.

In the FBI interrogation room, Alan Davis continued to spill his guts with impunity. Asked why he decided that then was the time to finally confess, he is said to have claimed it was never too late to make amends. Of course, it seemed to everyone that he was only remorseful once caught, and the question in such situations always remains the same: Are these types of criminals sorry for what they did, or just sorry they got found out?

It must also be considered that with Davis giving the prosecutors everything they wanted on Stanford's dealings, he was entering into a plea deal. If Allen Stanford were brought to justice, then Alan Davis would receive a much shorter sentence, so his sudden need to clear his conscience was anything but honourable. He was a con artist too, and no amount of 'grandfatherly' qualities would change that fact.

Laura Pendergest-Holt had taken the same path as her older lover, and a plea deal was agreed. Considering she seemed to struggle even with basic arithmetic, it is surprising that the FBI needed her confessions for anything other than damaging Stanford's character. By all accounts, the CFO of Stanford's empire really knew nothing about how the CDs and dodgy deals actually operated. Giving her a longer jail term for her part in ignoring it all and profiting greatly from it would have probably been a better move, but the FBI and SEC wanted Stanford more than anything, so maybe their decision was justified.

In February of 2009, the SEC amended its complaint to describe the alleged fraud as a "massive Ponzi scheme". The cat was well and truly out of the bag, and no amount of dressing it up as anything but a global fraud would work anymore. Stanford knew he was done, and with his only source of income linked to his banks—he had no personal accounts, only the money of others— any attempt at leaving the country would have been very hard.

With Stanford being Stanford, he genuinely believed all he had to do was show up at the police station and tell them they'd made a mistake, and it would all be over. But when he handed himself in on 8 June 2009, he did so in his last moments as a free man. The SEC had too much on him, and his old college pal had given the prosecutors everything they needed to send the Texan down for a long, long time.

Stanford reacted by requesting bail, and when this news broke, many big names and sports figures—including the golfer Vijay Singh—came forward to offer their support, both morally and financially. Fearing Stanford was now a flight risk, the prosecutors fought desperately to block any option of bail. Now that Stanford knew his lies most probably wouldn't work in a court of law, the SEC believed he would try and skip the country. Thankfully, their cries were heard by the judge. After turning up at his hearing wearing a snazzy suit and shouting to reporters that he would be out soon, Stanford was quickly denied bail and was taken to a local prison to be kept in pre-trial detention.

Locked up and with all his money unavailable, Stanford was forced to settle for a couple of state-appointed attorneys. Used to only the finest, this slap in the face of Stanford's pride and arrogance must have hurt, and he spent the first weeks of his incarceration changing his representation regularly. Finding someone capable enough to clear his name would have been an impossibility even with billions at his disposal, so his dismissal of the lawyers he saw as incompetent was wasted energy.

During his stay in prison, Stanford picked up where he had left off on the outside. In most penitentiaries, access to the phone is one of the most sought-after privileges afforded the prisoners. Stanford, a man who had always considered himself far more important than anyone else on the planet, took to monopolising the phone, sometimes spending hours on end calling lawyers, reporters, and anyone who would listen to his lies.

One of the prisoners finally snapped and severely beat Stanford, leaving him a bloody pulp on the ground. At one stage, it is said that the pint-sized inmate repeatedly slammed the head of his much larger victim into the concrete. Pictures and videos of Stanford's condition right after the paramedics had patched him up were quickly leaked to the press, but they didn't garner even a shred of the sympathy for him that his lawyers had hoped they would.

Being the type of opportunist and pathological liar he is, Stanford still saw an opportunity. With his head still in bandages, he told the judge and jury at his trial that he had suffered amnesia after the attack, and it broke his poor Texan heart to say it, but he wouldn't be able to give them the information they needed. Not surprisingly, he did remember that Alan Davis was behind the whole scheme and that his bit on the side, Miss Pendergest-Holt, was also guilty of fraud.

His trial had to be delayed, as he genuinely had taken quite a beating, but the amnesia claims were as fabricated as his stories of being a big football star back at Baylor.

Another dirty tactic followed when he told the judge that the prison doctor had prescribed him painkillers that were far too strong following the brutal assault, and now he was addicted. The physical and mental torture of his cravings had made him incapable of thinking about anything other than his cravings, and he was, therefore, unfit to stand trial.

The judge had to take his claims seriously, and there were traces of the painkiller in his system. Stanford managed to hold the trial off for several more months while he was weaned off the drug in the prison's medical facility. What he believed might change in the time spent between then and when the axe finally fell is impossible to know, but he probably still thought it would all work out in the end. It had to, right, as he was Robert Allen Stanford!

By the time the trial began, Stanford was running out of ideas, but he was still playing the victim card regarding the assault over use of the prison's phone. Throughout proceedings, he continually spat blood into a styrofoam cup as his lawyers demanded the judge show sympathy towards their client and his internal bleeding. Of course, Stanford's wounds had healed long before, and it turned out he had bitten the inside of his lip to produce the blood.

In the end, Stanford denied all charges against him and pleaded his innocence. Unfortunately for him, the testimonies of Alan

Davis and Laura Pendergest-Holt were too much for his lawyers to explain away. With the evidence acquired after his offices were raided and the severe lack of any real paperwork, the man who would still be known as Sir Allen for another few months yet was sinking fast. Still, he remained incredulous, often interrupting lawyers and stating his case throughout the trial.

Another damning piece of evidence—or rather, collection of evidence—was the endless reels of video tapes Stanford had commissioned his camera crew to film. As it turned out, he had made them record business meetings, lavish parties, interviews with employees, and even discussions about their CDs. His arrogance was actually starting to look like insanity in disguise, and it became fully evident he genuinely believed he was doing nothing wrong.

Stanford was finally brought up for sentencing in June of 2012, three years after handing himself in to the police. In a final desperate attempt to clear his name, despite everyone in attendance knowing he was going down, Stanford stood up and addressed the judge. He spoke of his loyalty to his clients, how all of the money was still sitting there waiting to be paid out, and that everything had been running smoothly until the FBI and SEC stuck their noses in and shook his investors' confidence in him.

The judge and jury dismissed his nonsense, and the man who flew a helicopter into Lord's was sentenced to 110 years in prison.

For their part in the scandal—and their cooperation with the prosecution—Alan Davis and Laura Pendergest-Holt received five and three years in prison, respectively. Given that Davis worked alongside Stanford for over two decades, handing out bribes, covering his partner's shady dealings, and defrauding over 300,000 people out of $8 million, his sentence couldn't even be considered a slap on the wrist. But the authorities had gotten the man they wanted and needed to ensure the evidence they had stuck to Stanford. Unfortunately, that meant thrashing out a plea bargain with a penis-enlarged criminal.

On 1 April 2010, the National Honours Committee of Antigua and Barbuda unanimously decided to strip Stanford of his knighthood. His insignia was removed from all records, yet his memory on the islands would be much harder to wash away. Losing his title must have hurt his ego, especially when the news was delivered to him as he sat in a cramped jail cell.

Robert Allen Stanford is currently seeing out his days in prison, and the odds of him ever getting even a sniff of a parole hearing are slim to none. Of course, he continues to spout his innocence in the ear of anyone who will listen, but when the cell door snaps shut at night and the prison lights are turned off, I wonder if he really believes his claims or just hopes someone else will?

Conclusion

The story of Robert Allen Stanford and his attempts to buy cricket is a strange one. The images of the stack of money and his helicopter landing on the grass at Lord's will be etched into the memories of the fans for eternity. But the story of his life is even more bizarre. From grunting loudly as he lifted weights in his own gyms to bringing all of his wives and girlfriends on holiday to Napa, Stanford did things his way.

Of course, his way turned out to be mostly illegal and always entertaining, but if we are to ever give him a shred of a compliment, the man knew what he wanted and went for it.

For those who he hurt and destroyed along the way, his tale is surely not as interesting a read as it is to the rest of us, and my heart genuinely goes out to them. But life is full of people and things that will sting you as you push through the undergrowth, and the trick is to dodge the pincers as best you can and learn from the times they do nip your leg.

Allen Stanford changed thousands of lives through the years—the vast majority for the worse—yet he never once apologised. I suppose this story is as much about the mind of people like him and the staggeringly selfish ways they work. Nothing is off-limits to a narcissist, and no amount of money will ever be enough for an egomaniac. Stanford believed he was entitled to other people's money. Why? Because he wanted to spend it, simple as that.

English and West Indies cricket lived on after the Twenty/20 for Twenty debacle, and the sport still continues to grow. Everyone makes mistakes, and the ECB made one giant, public one when they giggled and climbed into bed with Robert Allen Stanford. Did they ever own up to their gaff after everything fell apart? A little, but it always felt more like a passive-aggressive apology, like someone who knows they are in the wrong saying "I'm sorry you feel that way".

For the West Indian players who reinvested their winnings in SIB, it had all been for nothing. Like the other 300,000 people who had money in Stanford's care when the FBI and SEC raided his offices in Houston, their windfall became nothing but thin air. Stanford, Alan Davis, and all the other high rollers had spent it on themselves. They had drank it, eaten it, flown it, and stuck it in the panties of strippers in a nightclub decked out to look like Studio 54.

Even today, as Stanford lives out his life in prison, he continues to deny all wrongdoing. Whether he believes deep down that he'll one day be free, we'll never fully know, but on the face of things, at least, that is how it seems. But his claims of innocence mean nothing, as the whole house of cards was built with his hands. It is impossible for someone to put together a Ponzi scheme of that magnitude and remain oblivious.

When he stacked the board with yes men and women who had little to no financial background, he knew what he was doing. When he paid off regulators in Antigua and ordered Althea Crick fired, he knew what he was doing. And when he sent threatening letters to Charlie Rawl in an attempt to shake him down, he certainly knew what he was doing.

Allen Stanford chose his path and walked down it without ever looking back. For some, his sentence brings no personal justice, as they only see the life he lived before he was finally caught. Stanford had around three decades of being a billionaire through other people's savings, so seeing out the rest of his days in a cell might seem like he got the better end of the deal. Maybe if he admitted what he did and apologised, some of the pain of the investors would be eased, but that is all circumstantial now.

The boy who grew up wanting to emulate his grandfather never wanted to do things small. He wanted everything and more, and there were never going to be enough laws or ethical dilemmas to stop him. For one thing, he simply dodged the laws, and when they became too stringent for his liking, he moved to a place where they were easier to bend. As for ethics, he possessed none, so they were never going to be a problem.

At the time of his $20 million cricket game, Stanford was already in trouble, and he knew it. Deciding to throw himself into the world's spotlight by making such a show at Lord's speaks volumes of the man's character. To think that someone who surely knew the Feds were looking into their dealings believed that flashing a stack of cash in a Perspex box was a good idea is nearly impossible to comprehend. Yet Stanford must have seen some benefit to it all.

Going back through the life of Allen Stanford is a journey full of shocks, bewilderment, and, yes, a lot of laughs. In hindsight, we can say people should have seen through him, but unlike Charles Ponzi, the returns Allen offered his investors seemed genuinely legitimate at first glance. Also, when anyone wanted their money, they usually got it—after they couldn't be convinced to reinvest—so everything always seemed above board.

Now, we can look back and wonder how on Earth he could get away with it all, but money has a funny way of blinding people, and when Sir Allen built another hospital in Antigua or showed people around his offices in Houston with the pictures on the walls of him shaking George Bush's hand, everyone bought into the show. Never forget that Stanford was a master manipulator and a world-class thief. He knew the way people's minds worked, and he had all the tricks and smokescreens to shepherd them into a position of trust.

His spending was outrageous, to say the least, and the arrogance he showed in flashing his wealth is the stuff of Hollywood movies. Yet he maintained his position as guardian of 300,000 investors' money for 3 decades, so he was good at what he did, at least in the sense of fooling people. Would his life have turned out differently if he'd stuck to running gyms and buying up depressed real estate? It's very doubtful, as the riches he achieved doing that would never have been enough. To make insane amounts of money fast, he needed a scheme, and boy did he create one.

I think the only way to see this book out is to do so with a quote from the man himself, and it sums up his narcissism and life views perfectly: "I always lived very frugally. I flew around on a private jet and I had a boat. But I always lived very frugally" (Pressler, 2009).

References

Bull, A. (2008, October 28). Profiteering vulgarity: Just how cricket used to be. The Guardian. https://www.theguardian.com/sport/blog/2008/oct/26/stanford-super-series-cricket

Churcher, S. (2009, March 1). Revealed: The secret of Sir Allen Stanford's three "outside wives." Mail Online. https://www.dailymail.co.uk/news/article-1158169/Revealed-The-secret-Sir-Allen-Stanfords-outside-wives.html

Darby, M. (1998). In Ponzi we trust. Smithsonian Magazine. https://www.smithsonianmag.com/history/in-ponzi-we-trust-64016168/

Dealbook. (2011). What's the holdup in the Stanford case? DealBook. https://archive.nytimes.com/dealbook.nytimes.com/2011/05/05/whats-the-holdup-in-the-stanford-case/

Driver, A. (2012, January 31). Stanford sought to influence regulator. Reuters. https://www.reuters.com/article/us-stanford-trial-idUSTRE80T1PU20120131

Flintoff, A. (2009) Ashes to Ashes: One Test After Another. Autobiography. https://www.amazon.co.uk/Andrew-Flintoff-Ashes-After-Another/dp/0340951567

Hayter, P. (2009, February 21). Special report: Stanfordgate - England cricket chiefs' dealings with Sir Allen under scrutiny. Mail Online. https://www.dailymail.co.uk/sport/cricket/article-1151827/Special-report-Stanfordgate--England-cricket-chiefs-dealings-Sir-Allen-scrutiny.html

Ishmael, S M. (2009, September 25). Allen Stanford: Puppet Master by Freddie Flintoff. The Financial Times. https://www.ft.com/content/b8491dad-98c7-3bd3-b5f1-8cdf7926893b

James, G. (2022, February 21). BBC Radio 5 Live - Sport's Strangest Crimes, Allen Stanford - The Man Who Bought Cricket. BBC. https://www.bbc.co.uk/programmes/p09wqmpd#:~:text=Money%20laundering%2C%20the%20FBI%2C%20drug

Johns, N. (2022, February 4). Allen Stanford: The American who bought cricket's soul in the Caribbean. The Irish Times. https://www.irishtimes.com/sport/other-sports/allen-stanford-the-american-crook-who-bought-cricket-s-soul-in-the-caribbean-1.4787826

Newman, P. (2009, September 24). FREDDIE FLINTOFF UNCUT: We were Allen Stanford's puppets, only there for his millions. Mail Online. https://www.dailymail.co.uk/sport/cricket/article-1215685/FREDDIE-FLINTOFF-UNCUT-We-Allen-Stanfords-puppets-millions.html

Pressler, J. (2009, April 7). "I've always lived very frugally," Says Robert Allen Stanford. Intelligencer. https://nymag.com/intelligencer/2009/04/robert_allen_stanford_is_going.html

sidbreakball. (2016, January 12). When a Knight landed a helicopter filled with cash at Lords Stadium. Www.sportskeeda.com. https://www.sportskeeda.com/cricket/a-knight-landed-helicopter-filled-cash-lords-stadium

Sportsmail. (2008, October 31). Botham: England should forget row and just get out and enjoy Stanford match. Mail Online. https://www.dailymail.co.uk/sport/cricket/article-

1082077/Botham-England-forget-controversy-concentrate-
winning-big-Stanford-showdown.html

Printed in Great Britain
by Amazon